Death of Lord Percy

An Aristocratic Sleuths Mystery

by

David Wilson

Copyright © 2019 by David Wilson

For information, email Cozy Cat Press, cozycatpress@aol.com or visit our website at: www.cozycatpress.com

COZY CAT
PRESS

ISBN: 978-1-946063-97-7
Printed in the United States of America

10 9 8 7 6 5 4 3 2 1

To my wife, Tess, who gave me the encouragement and confidence to write. She tells me I have a mind like Lord Bigsby while she has a much more intelligent mind like Field Marshal James.

CHAPTER ONE

After arriving home from Nepal, Lord Bigsby and I received the highest praise from Field Marshal Sir Watt Courage for the way we had conducted ourselves while we were there, and for offering help to the Gurkhas and others who were living at a subsistence level. He said the king had told him how we had acquiesced to his plea of leading by example in not drinking alcohol during our visit, but he said he'd viewed this with a little skepticism!

Both Bigsby and I had retired from the army, apart from acting in an ambassadorial capacity just a few times a year. Our next assignment would be a visit to Canada to thank the troops for their service to the British Army and to try and encourage some of the younger generation to join. We would be recounting some of our own more memorable experiences for this purpose.

No date had been planned yet for our trip there and my friend Bigsby and I were spending more and more time at The Club in Mayfair, where we were both members, with the occasional game of Polo. We knew we were starting to drink too much and with all the fine dining we'd been doing, we were putting on weight and our fitness was beginning to suffer. After being accustomed to so much action and adventure in our lives, we were getting bored and desperately needed some kind of interest.

Bigsby had certainly surprised me the previous evening while we were lunching at The Club. He told me that the secretary the previous week had told him that a well-spoken gentleman had been asking if he knew anyone with integrity and compassion who would be prepared to undertake an urgent private investigation. He said his first thoughts were that *we* had all the necessary qualities with our eccentricities and knowledge.

My friend, Bigsby, is a well-built, fatherly figure with black, curly unkempt hair who can be instantly recognized by his walrus moustache who, when out, often sports a colourful bow-tie, plus fours and a white panama hat. I myself am a tall, slender person with a studious look and, when out, I always sport a bowler hat, my regimental tie, and Cambridge blazer of which I am so proud. We are an eccentric pair indeed and once seen, never forgotten!

We are both friendly, compassionate people and after seeing so many atrocities during our army days, we realize the great need for peace rather than war and for love rather than hatred.

"Let's start a private detective agency together, James," he said, "purely on an amateur basis. The more I think about the prospect, the more excited I get. We're men of action and we're both missing the exhilaration and excitement that the Army gave us."

I didn't think he was serious at first but the look on his face told me he was, and he asked me to think it over. He said we'd have a great advantage over most agencies as he had influential contacts if ever they were needed.

I became very intrigued with his proposition and it began to appeal to me greatly. With Bigsby's contacts I was sure we would only have the upper class clients and our expenses wouldn't be a financial burden for them. This meant that we need only accept those cases that appealed to us and aroused our curiosity.

My only concern was that I'd be left with all the initial work of searching for clues from the information provided by our clients. Bigsby was sometimes a great help in this respect as he often used illogical logic which tended to put my mind on a different train of thought which then helped point us in the right direction. He excelled on the rifle range and sports field at Oxford while I gained first-class honours at Cambridge; we complemented each other perfectly.

I would be meeting Bigsby at The Club in an hour's time, but I had more or less made up my mind about his proposition. Everyone at The Club had evidently been remarking for the last few weeks that Bigsby and I no longer entered into our usual banter and our frequent laughter hadn't been heard much. Bigsby had told me the previous week that he was so bored that he'd even taken to washing the dishes at home—but after breaking two of the most expensive serving plates, his wife had banned him from the kitchen. She also demanded a new dinner service from one of the most prestigious London shops and this had cost him a small fortune. Bigsby washing the dishes!! Unheard of—even when he was in the Army!

We had been friends for most of our lives and we were well known for our ripostes and good-humoured teasing. In all the years we'd known each other and spent together in the Army, we'd never argued in the slightest. Thinking of my dear friend in such a perilous state made up my mind.

I arrived at The Club about an hour late and there he was with his favourite meal of duck barely touched and the wine bottle unopened. Never had I seen my friend in such a dejected state. I tried to cheer him up with a joke. "What did Detective Duck say to his partner?" When there was no flicker of emotion on his face, I said, "Let's quack the case." When I continued, "Let's start tomorrow," his whole demeanour changed.

"Do you really mean it, James?" he said with the twinkle back in his eyes and, after looking so depressed and haggard for a few weeks, he was suddenly transformed to his normal state.

"What did the policeman say to his belly button, James? You're under a vest! Ha! Ha!" What a transformation! And it made me so happy that I'd agreed to join him in his planned detective agency.

"What a friend you are, James! Let's open the claret and drink to the success of our new venture."

I was wondering how long it would be before we were up and running and able to advertise for clients but I didn't have to wait long before I got an answer.

"I was so sure, James, that you would partner with me that everything is legally prepared for us to start tomorrow. We only have to sign the documents and we're ready to go. I was advised that even as amateurs we need to be covered for every eventuality."

Bigsby was now unrecognizable from the dismal, uncommunicative figure of the last few weeks. "Let's advertise in *The London Chronicle* tonight as this is the newspaper read by the aristocracy. I'll leave it to your greater knowledge to design an advert for the paper and arrange for one hundred business cards to be printed."

Lord Bigsby and Field Marshal James
Eton and Oxbridge Educated
Private Detectives for the Aristocracy
Amateurs—No Fees
Confidentiality Assured
Address: The Club, Mayfair

"I've drawn this up for our business cards. What do you think about it?"

"That's perfect, James. It shows how well educated we both are and being schooled at Eton shows that our families were very wealthy and of high social standing in life. We may charge no fees, James, but our expenses will be high as we cannot lower our everyday living standard! Our Army pension and our investments add up to more than we'll ever need financially so we can look at our enterprise as an enjoyable and exciting pastime."

I was about to ask more details about our new venture when Bigsby got up and asked me to follow him. He led me to a small room by the side of the bar and ushered me in. I gasped! There was a large table with two seats behind it, an impressive ink well, a blotter and sheets of paper laid neatly on the desk. In fact, everything a prospective detective agency needs.

"I couldn't stop thinking about becoming an amateur detective ever since the secretary mentioned it to me. I've prepared everything I could possibly think of as I was so sure you'd agree to join me. I even managed to persuade The Club manager to allow us to use a room right next to the bar. How can one possibly think without the finest of wines close at hand? With the advert in the paper tonight I'm sure our first client will be with us tomorrow.

Members of the upper class would not debase themselves in asking help from inferiors but would trust implicitly those of their own standing. I wonder what they'll think when we outline our expenses. A first-class hotel if it's necessary to be away from home, the finest of food and wine as well as a few purchases for ourselves and our wives which we deem essential to the case! What do you think, James, my friend?"

"An excellent idea, and very logical, if I may say so. To take presents back for our wives is an obligation which we cannot ignore. It's said a fool and his money are soon parted!"

"My wife is now demanding a new dining table and chairs, but I think, James, that anything of that nature may well be questioned by our clients."

"Do you know why dough is another word for money, Bigsby? Because everyone kneads it!! Ha! Ha!"

Following a wonderful lunch, it was time for me to get busy. After agreeing to meet Bigsby at The Club at ten o'clock the following morning, I raced to the offices of *The London Chronicle* which promised to put in our advert that evening as a special favour and free of charge. My next stop was at the printers who hoped to have our business cards ready within two days. With a happy heart and excitement mounting within me, I made my way back home. My wife was certainly happy to see me back to my old self.

I was at The Club well before ten o'clock the following morning with Bigsby already ensconced in the bigger red leather chair. You get nothing for guessing who was taking the role of the boss. We'd been discussing our roles in the business for ten minutes when a sharp rap came on the door.

"Come in please. Lord Bigsby and Field Marshal James here," said Bigsby in a formal voice. The door opened and in walked a tall, slender and bearded middle-aged man about our own age. He had a determined, arrogant look and no smile ever seemed to have crossed his face.

"Good morning, Lord Bigsby and Sir James. I'm relying on you to help me find my daughter. You've started up your agency at a perfect time for me as there's no way I could have trusted those lower class scoundrels who call themselves private detectives."

"Good morning, sir, and we will do everything in our power to help you. We call our first meeting with our clients a preliminary hearing to enable us to assess the case put before us. James will now proceed to ask you the questions he deems as relevant. Could you please introduce yourself?"

"My name is Sir Martin Nash, and my daughter has been missing for four weeks. I was hoping she would have made contact by now but there's been no word from her. My wife and I are awfully concerned about what may have happened."

"Could you please give us as much information as possible, Sir Martin, about your daughter and if you think there could be a possible reason for her disappearance? Any information, however trivial you think it may be, could be of the utmost importance."

"Her name is Priscilla Fairdown, aged twenty, and unmarried. We last saw her on the fourth of May, about ten o'clock in the evening, which is approximately four weeks ago. We are both in great distress as she is our only child."

"Could you please let us know about her education, interests and friends?"

"Our darling studied music at London University where she gained a first class honours and thence went on to achieve a Master's Degree in the same subject. Earlier this year, she began her thesis for her Doctorate. She only has a handful of friends and no real pastimes."

I could see Bigsby getting very exasperated, but I secretly motioned for him to stay silent. This was like getting blood from a stone. I continued with my questioning but I decided not to press too hard for information.

"Sir Martin, could you please give us a little idea as to her interests, however minimal these may be, and what kind of friends she mixes with? If you have any idea where she might be, could you please provide us with this information?"

"Priscilla has three friends, of whom none are very close, of her own social standing but to divulge their names would be a severe breach of protocol. Her only interest, apart from music, is art. She enjoys still-life and portrait painting, but she only has the talent of a reasonably good amateur. Priscilla has been saying for the last year that her immediate passion in life was to go to France to enable her to do a collection of paintings of the Pyrenees and to become more acquainted with the French artists and composers but, unfortunately, I didn't have the funds to support her. This took me by complete surprise as her ability as a landscape artist is virtually zero."

"That will be all for now, Sir Martin, and we'll undoubtedly take on your case but it's more than likely to be a case of a rebellious young graduate staying with friends until she returns back to her senses. All you need to do now is to leave us your home address and to agree that you'll be willing to reimburse us for all our expenses. We have to warn you that these may be considerable but, as complete amateurs and novices, we don't charge a fee. We will contact you as soon as we have any further information."

"Yes, this I will acquiesce to and I totally agree, James, about the reason you gave for her disappearance. I'll bid you good-day and I'll hopefully hear from you in the not too distant future."

CHAPTER TWO

"Why did the dishonest man grow a beard, James?"

"I don't know but I'm sure we were speaking to one a few moments ago."

"So that no one could call him a bare-faced liar! Ha! Ha!"

"You may have hit the nail on the head there. It would be a good idea, if you're able, to find out as much as you can about him through one of your most trusted contacts and see if you can get to know what time he returns home from his employment in the evening. I believe it's important that I have a word with his wife alone. I deduce it will be to our advantage if her husband's not aware of my visit and is not present so, hopefully, she'll feel more free to speak."

"I couldn't agree more. If I hadn't known you better I would have classified you as one of the worst interrogators I've ever witnessed. You may now enlighten me as to your reason why."

"There's definitely much more to this case than meets the eye. I'm under the impression that he knows you as a person who's not very well educated academically, and I wanted to give him the impression that I was the same. It appears to me that he wanted to hire someone to find his daughter but who didn't possess the brains to look at the case a little deeper. I'm also of the opinion that he has no affection for his daughter, but we'll see."

"A light refreshment of partridge cooked in red wine with chanterelles, washed down with a little burgundy is now called for, James, and then I'll try to hunt down my contacts to find out more about Sir Martin Nash. I don't recall the name."

After our meal, which was much more than a light refreshment, Bigsby went off to the Fellows Club to locate one of his trusted contacts. I stayed alone in the bar, deep in thought, with an occasional sip of wine. Gradually I dozed off to sleep and this is how Bigsby found me on his return.

"Wake up, James; we're on a serious case."

"You know what they say, Bigsby. Sleep is the most wonderful experience there is, apart from drink, and looking at that empty wine bottle, it appears that I have partaken of both. How did your search for information go?"

"Sir Martin, as we assumed, was of the middle-class who was educated at an inferior private school but, because of his brilliant academic mind, won a scholarship to Oxford where he gained a first-class honours in the history of art, a Master's degree in the same subject and a Doctorate for which he wrote a thesis on 'Economics in the International Art World'. In other words, he was a genius. His ambition was to establish an auction house to rival the greatest names but he lacked the capital and the practical know-how to do so.

"His first venture, which was financed mainly by his father, was set to flourish until funds unexpectedly dried up. This took the city by surprise. He attempted to raise money, thereafter, by starting various enterprises but all failed as he didn't possess the practical know-how or the essential contacts to make them succeed. My contact told me that he would have made a brilliant business partner as his ideas were often of genius proportions but he was determined to prove to the aristocracy that he could go it alone.

"He may have tried to raise capital through dubious means, but my contacts haven't heard of any serious criminality in his dealings, although they have heard very little about him during the last two years. He usually arrives home a little after six o'clock so you'd better start off at once to have a meeting with his wife. His wife was previously married to Lord Percy, the well-known artist, who died a couple of years ago in mysterious circumstances. Apart from that, my contact knows virtually nothing about her as she has always appeared to live a quiet, happy, contented and homely life."

Thus, I set off to visit Sir Martin's wife being none the wiser how I should approach the subject of her husband's visit. I decided not to worry and take everything as it came.

As I walked down the Strand, the pavement now full of shoppers and theatre-goers, I reminisced what it would have been like when Charles Dickens had lived here over one hundred years ago. Passing the Houses of Parliament, I looked up at Big Ben which a few moments earlier had chimed the hour of four o'clock. The largest and most accurate four-faced striking and chiming clock in the world, and the symbol of British democracy, stood out prominently on the London skyline.

A few moments later, I arrived at Lady Helen's home overlooking the River Thames. It was an imposing stone-built house of neo-gothic design with a large well-tended garden. The flowering cherry trees by the gate were starting to blossom and ivy covered much of the front of the house.

A maid came to the door and I handed her our business card to take to her Lady. I was told to wait in the hall where I was surprised to find myself surrounded by some of the finest landscape paintings I'd ever seen. A few of the paintings appeared to be of the Pyrenees, but what truly caught my suspicious mind was a picture hook on which no painting hung.

I was eventually ushered into the lounge where I was given a very warm and friendly greeting. I was expecting the room to be finely furnished with expensive furniture and antiques, but this was a lived in, homely room with well-worn chairs and a settee with a few more of Sir Percy's paintings adorning the walls. The one luxurious item in the room was a mahogany and maple Steinway grand piano which must have cost a small fortune.

Lady Helen was a stylish, elegant lady with a ready smile and all the traits of a fine upbringing. She was casually dressed in a plain brown tweed skirt matched with a red sweater.

"I am so pleased you have come when I'm alone so that I can tell you my greatest concern, but please make no mention of this to Martin as he would only accuse me of over-reacting. My mind is so confused and I need someone I can trust to pour out my worries and fears to.

"I am certain Percy was murdered, but I haven't the slightest idea why. He was a very quiet, extremely kind and compassionate man and I know of no one who would even dislike him. For this reason alone, I've been getting more convinced every day that his death was, in some way, connected to his visits to the Pyrenees. He told us very little about these visits, and for this reason, I didn't like to ask.

"Perhaps I'm becoming paranoid due to the worry of his unexplained death. I know I've always been an over-protective mother and I constantly worry that Priscilla, being Percy's daughter, may also be in danger. Please, if you do find her in France, persuade her to come home at once. I'm still finding it hard to come to terms with the fact that Percy is no longer with us and if anything happens to Priscilla I'll be devastated."

"We will do everything in our power to help, Lady Helen, but please don't worry too much."

"My present husband knew Lord Bigsby at Oxford, as they had met on the rugby field, and he'd heard that his intelligence was lacking somewhat. When he saw your advert in the paper he advised me that your agency was the best place to go as he was sure Lord Bigsby had the contacts to find my daughter, but wouldn't have the intelligence to pry deeper. My husband was unaware that I knew of your academic achievements at Cambridge and some of your brilliant exploits together during the war."

"Thank you for such kind words, my Lady, but could you please advise me of your name and as much about yourself and your family as you feel free to do at the moment and anything you know that may help us to find Priscilla. Confidentiality will be assured."

"My parents were the Duke and Duchess of Artfield who were landowners in the south-east of England and endowed with much wealth. My late husband was the Marquis of Fairdown who was better known as the highly celebrated artist Percy

Fairdown, or Lord Percy as he was affectionately known, and this is his family home.

"I am now the Marchioness of Fairdown, but known to all my friends as Lady Helen. I, myself, am also a well-known portrait artist. Our beloved daughter, Priscilla, studied music at London University and is now studying for a doctorate. She was offered a scholarship at Cambridge, but declined as she's a very quiet and reserved person with old-fashioned ideals although she is possessed of a great sense of humour. That she has not acquired our talent in the artistic field upsets her greatly and even with the tuition of her late father, her progression was only moderate."

"Thank you for this information, Lady Helen. It would be a great honour for me to listen to one of Priscilla's renditions on the Steinway one day if we are successful in tracing her. How did you meet your present husband, if you don't mind me asking?"

"My late husband had passed away about six months previously and I was still grieving for him as was my daughter also. We were such a close and happy family and spent many carefree days together in the countryside. We were all so much at home there and we'd been looking for a suitable home in the Cotswolds where we could spend some of our vacations when he died. Priscilla hated London but loved the freedom of the countryside.

"I met Martin one day at Sotheby's while I was looking for quality picture frames for my late husband's unframed work, and he appeared to be a very knowledgeable and friendly person. I soon realized that he was well below my social status and that he'd be hoping I would finance him in his desire to start an auction house that would grow into one which would become internationally acclaimed. Social status doesn't worry me at all and I knew I was deeply in love with him. He appeared, also, to dote on my daughter. We married six months after we first met and have now been man and wife for one year. To think Percy has been dead now for two years and I'm no wiser about the reason why.

"Martin told me his frustration in being unable to start a successful business was because of lack of finance and practical knowledge. He said that some of his past financial dealings had been a little dodgy but all this had come about through severe frustration.

"I persuaded him that his expertise was in the academic field and that he should seek employment as an art expert at a reputable auction house where I was sure his talent would blossom. Shortly after our marriage, a position of senior valuer arose at the Peregrino International Auction Services where my late husband always auctioned his works of art and was held in very high esteem. With Martin's qualifications and a reference from myself, he was accepted for the post and he started work immediately.

"We've been very happy in our life but the worry of my late husband's sudden and unexplained death still haunts me. That's all I'm free to say before I broach the subject with my husband and decide on the best course of action. I'm sure I'll be arranging another meeting with yourself and Lord Bigsby very soon."

"Lady Helen, before I forget, I noticed in the hall that there's a picture missing from one of the picture-hooks. Could you please tell me if you think this may have any relevance to your daughter's disappearance?"

"It possibly could, Field Marshal James, as it's one of Priscilla's favourites which my late husband had painted on his final trip to Lourdes. There's a strong possibility that she may have taken it with her when she went. I do have a rough sketch of it which I'll go and get for you now."

After she had handed me the sketch, I wished her good-day and left to report my conversation to Bigsby.

"Here you are at last! I was worrying you'd been kidnapped. There's an article in the *London Gazette* on the kind of food that we may be served in a high-class French hotel and I discovered why the French eat snails. They don't like fast food! Ha! Give me a quick rundown of what took place and then we can dine in peace. I'm scared of dining at home in the evening at the moment because Lady Bigsby uses those expensive plates. My hands tremble when I eat as I'm so afraid that I may break one."

I gave Bigsby an account of the conversation with Lady Helen and told him I was sure we'd see her again and that she appeared to regard her late husband's death as suspicious. I asked him what his thoughts were on the case so far but he responded in typical fashion.

"What I do know is that a case of Chablis arrived last night and The Club is putting on a special lunch tomorrow of pheasant roasted in pear juice with chanterelles. We can't miss a luxury like that, James. What conjecture have you arrived at, my good friend?"

"There are two unusual details which stand out to me. Firstly, it does seem surprising that Priscilla hasn't acquired any of the renowned talent of her parents, but this has more than likely been offset with her musical ability. Secondly, I'm sure that the sketch of the painting which Lady Helen gave me, of a young lady sitting in her wheelchair outside a palatial-looking building, holds the key to the whereabouts of Priscilla.

"Lady Helen was quite sure that Priscilla took the original painting from the hall before she disappeared. Surmising that she did take the painting, it seems likely that she knows roughly where it was painted. I wouldn't be surprised if the location was Lourdes or in that vicinity. That's where Lady Helen's late husband spent much of his time painting, without his family."

"That appears to be a very reasonable assumption, James. I have a couple of contacts who spend holidays in that area so I'll go in the morning to see if I can glean any information from them."

I arrived at our office a little late the next morning, where I was handed a note to say that Lady Helen and her husband would be arriving for a meeting with us at eleven o'clock unless we had any prior arrangements. Bigsby, I assumed, had gone to see if any of his contacts could shed any light on where the building in the painting was situated. I decided to have coffee and put my feet up while reading the newspaper to see what else was going on in the world. A few minutes before eleven, Bigsby arrived back with a gleam of success in his eyes.

CHAPTER THREE

"It looks like I've been the only one working this morning, James. Is there anything new happening in the world at the moment, if you believe what's written in the newspapers?"

"Great success. My first contact, a mountaineer who loved climbing in the Pyrenees, recognized the building as a small orphanage in Lourdes. He was asked to give a talk there a couple of years ago about his climbing adventures and he was much impressed. It appeared to him more like a home than an orphanage as the few children who were there all received the best personal attention. He remembers clearly seeing a disabled young lady, exceptionally talented at art, who had been given individual tuition by a peer of the realm from England. I was told he was a well-known artist, enjoying a holiday at that time."

"The English peer would surely not be Lord Percy, or would it? How many peers do you know, Bigsby, who are recognized artists?"

"It appeared that all leads, however tenuous they may be, pointed us towards Lourdes. I immediately thought of our stay at the Chateau de Pois with General Couture during the war a few years previously."

Bigsby was referring to a time when he'd received a bravery award for saving the life of a sheep stuck in a barbed wire fence which some stupid idiot in the War Department had interpreted as saving the life of Private Lamb under intense bombardment from the enemy. I have to admit that Bigsby did exaggerate just a little! The food at the Chateau was second to none and I was sincerely hoping we could dine there again one evening if France was indeed our destination.

A knock at the office door disturbed my thoughts and Lady Helen and Sir Martin greeted us with much aplomb. Bigsby motioned them to be seated before speaking.

"Could you please give us all the information available to you, however trivial it may seem, that may help us find your daughter? At the moment, we do have one avenue which we are considering exploring further."

Helen and Martin looked at each other tenderly before Helen spoke. "We've been talking matters over and we would like you—Lord Bigsby and Field Marshal James—to continue to search for our daughter and also to widen your investigation to include the death of my late husband which I regard as extremely suspicious, even though Martin tried to assure me that there was no cause for concern and that he'd have preferred the investigation to be confined to locating Priscilla. The doctors were baffled by his cause of death but eventually they put it down to natural causes. I'm sure they still have grave doubts but they took the easy way out. Are you sure you don't charge any fee?"

"Lady Helen, we can assure you that we only charge the amount that's spent during the course of our investigation. We are both compassionate, family loving people and we look forward to reuniting you both with Priscilla. We also agree to inquire into the death of Lord Percy as it appears that the disappearance of your daughter and the death of your late husband may be connected in some way. Could you please let us know a little more about your late husband and his career as an artist and any reason you know for your daughter's disappearance?"

"My husband was a very talented, respected and highly acclaimed landscape artist. Apart from spending a few weeks a year painting in the area of the Pyrenees, his paintings were of the countryside in England.

"He would go over to the Pyrenees three times a year for a fortnight each time and always returned with six stunning paintings which sold at auction, almost immediately, for exceedingly high prices. He donated the profits from these paintings to a children's charity in France. This was totally in character with Percy as he was such a kind, generous and loving man. He insisted that he travelled abroad alone so that he could concentrate fully on his work. He always came home a revitalized person. I have no idea why my daughter disappeared, other than she missed her father so much."

"As far as you are aware, did your daughter ever go to France with your late husband or have you any suspicions of her doing so?"

"Not as far as I know, Field Marshal James, but she was away from home for one week during my late husband's last visit to France before he died and it's possible she could have gone there but she made no intimation to myself of the matter. This would have been slightly over two years ago.

"A couple of months ago, she casually mentioned to me that she'd like to visit Lourdes to enable her to see the area of the Pyrenees which her father loved so much. I only recalled her saying this when I noticed, last night, that her passport was missing from her room."

"That's all the questions I have for the moment, but could you please provide us with an up-to-date picture of your daughter and your late husband? Ah, Lady Helen, something that has just at this moment occurred to me. Could you kindly tell me when Priscilla was born and if she has spent all her life in London or has she lived elsewhere at any time?"

"Priscilla was born in London on the fourth of April, twenty years ago. I was taken to the intensive care unit immediately after her birth, because of minor complications, and it was about four hours until I saw my daughter. She was a beautiful baby and she has retained that beauty until this day. She has received all her education here also. The only times she has left the city have been on family vacations and the one week away where she could possibly have visited France, as I mentioned earlier."

It was agreed that Sir Martin would provide the pictures for us before the end of the day. He had nothing further to add to his wife's information although he affirmed that he fully supported her.

Immediately after they had left, the restaurant manager came to tell us that our meal of pheasant was ready and the Chablis had sufficiently chilled. Bigsby's face lit up and with the greatest alacrity I had seen from him for some time, he was off his chair and heading for the dining room. When we were both seated, he asked me what I thought our next step should be.

"This pheasant looks wonderful, my Lord. Do you know why birds fly south in the winter? Because it's too far to walk! Ha! The next step is for you to contact General Couture, to see if he can find suitable accommodation for us near Lourdes. There seems to be a reasonable chance that we might find Priscilla there."

General Couture, a great friend of ours from our army days, is an athletic-looking man who is always fashionably dressed. He's regarded as one of the most able French commanders and his men hold him in high regard.

"I wholeheartedly agree with you, James, but we do need accommodation that's of the same high standard as the Chateau du Pais. I'll contact General Couture immediately after our meal. We can't be expected to work on such a complex case without good food and wine to sustain us."

What a meal it was and surely one of the best meals we'd eaten at The Club. "We'd better take an hour's rest now, James, before our preparations to leave for France."

After Couture had been contacted, we made all the arrangements necessary for our journey. Couture responded almost immediately to say that his friend owned a Chateau very close to Lourdes which possessed an excellent reputation and would ensure that our specialties would be included on the menu. He also promised to meet us at the station at Lourdes on our arrival as he was off duty for a couple of days. We were both so much looking forward to meeting up with him again.

Sir Martin had already sent us the photos and by five o'clock in the evening we began our journey to the Pyrenees. Although we didn't believe it was necessary, Bigsby took his trusty Walther while I armed myself with the khukuri that was given to me by the Gurkhas.

It was a long journey to the Chateau de Champs but during our army days we had become well accustomed to travel. Having our luggage with us for our stay in France, we took a taxi to Waterloo station from where we would proceed to Southampton to board the passenger ferry going to Cherbourg.

Looking up at the impressive three-story Victory Arch with its statue for peace over the entrance to the station which was constructed to commemorate the railway employees who lost their lives during the first world war, brought back poignant memories for me. I remembered those soldiers with courage and bravery that few could comprehend. Many saw comrades blown to pieces and heard the anguished cries of those in mortal agony resounding in their ears. They collected the scattered remains of those blown to pieces—a shattered head, a foot, an arm being gathered together for burial. *For those who survived the war how haunting the memories must be*, I thought.

Our journey to Southampton was uneventful. The ferry was already docked, so we boarded for our journey across the English Channel, passing our time after enjoying a hearty lunch, either reading or sleeping.

Before long, we could see the outline of Cherbourg. It had been a military port during the war which now boasted a major shipbuilding industry. Here was where the 'unsinkable' Titanic had docked for the penultimate time before hitting an iceberg on that fateful day in 1912, with the loss of over fifteen hundred lives. What a tragedy.

We had a couple of hours to spare before our train left from Cherbourg to Lourdes on the final leg of our journey so I went to see the impressive monument to Napoleon in which he is sitting astride a horse. Bigsby, as usual, went for a tour of the wine shops and returned with a couple of bottles of vintage claret to devour on our six hundred mile journey to Lourdes.

Eventually, it was time for us to board the train which would take us through Paris and then onwards to the picturesque university town of Poitiers before arriving at Lourdes. For the first time since leaving London, I mentioned the subject of finding Priscilla.

"I'm sure, Bigsby, that we'll find Priscilla at Lourdes. Lourdes is the only place where she's travelled alone and, according to Lady Helen, she took her passport with her when she left home. Now, open that bottle of claret and let's have a couple of glasses before we take a rest."

"A great idea, James, and then I'm going to sleep."

Thirty minutes later, the stentorious roar of Bigsby snoring could be heard. Fortunately, I was so accustomed to the noise from our Army days that this didn't bother me, and I, too, was soon sound asleep.

We were only a few miles from our destination when we woke totally refreshed. On our arrival, our old friend, General Couture, was waiting to meet us and drive us to our hotel. We greeted each other like the old friends we were, being happy to be re-united.

"What brings you here in such haste, my dear friends, Bigsby and James? Are you on a holiday trip or on some kind of business? Whichever way, I'm so glad to see you both again. I knew you would need transport so I've hired a 1921 yellow Citroen B2 10HP Torpedo for your use while you're in France. If I can be of assistance in any way, I will be honoured to help."

Bigsby's face was something to behold.

"What a car, Couture! You know how much I love driving and I'll really enjoy driving this. I can't wait to get behind the wheel! Do you know where it was produced?"

"These cars, Bigsby, are produced by Citroen at their famous factory in the Quai de Javel, just five minutes from the Eiffel Tower. I knew how thrilled you'd be."

"It's nearly time for our evening meal so let's eat first and then we'll explain to you why we thought it necessary to come to Lourdes," replied Bigsby.

What a magnificent place it was. Bigsby said we'd refer to it as *Champs* as this was simpler to say. It was both a working vineyard and a high class hotel.

Even Bigsby, who didn't know the difference between Elizabethan and Tudor design, was impressed with the French Renaissance architecture of the Chateau. With turrets on each of its four corners and an impressive arched entrance, the building surely mirrored the rebirth of classical culture. The immense grounds of mixed woodland and rich grassland, with the vineyards on the slopes behind, was a haven for wildlife. Lavender and poppies were in abundance and I spotted a variety of orchids, including my favourite—yellow bee orchid.

A pair of red-rumped swallows were building their nest under the turrets, a crested-tit was feeding on the nuts at the bird-table, a honey buzzard was gliding overhead and a nightingale could be clearly heard with its powerful and soothing song.

We'd booked into the hotel for two nights as we were expecting it would be relatively easy to find Lady Helen's daughter and that we'd also have enough time to tour the vineyard and sample the wine. I had no theory as yet regarding the death of Lord Percy. There was no indication there'd be any connection with the Pyrenees.

We had no reason to believe that, if we were able to find Priscilla, her life would be in danger but we thought it advisable, for Lady Helen's peace of mind, that we do all we could to persuade her daughter to come back to London with us.

After a superb meal of beef fillet, roast potatoes and ceps, and a bottle of claret, we explained to Couture the reason for our visit. We then retired to bed to prepare ourselves for an early start to Lourdes the following morning. It was wonderful to see Bigsby so full of life again and back to his own self. He must have been very depressed to reach the point of even considering washing dishes for his wife!

We left after breakfast for Lourdes with Couture accompanying us. We considered it wise for him to come in case there was unexpected trouble which required the assistance of the law and also as an independent witness.

What a majestic place it is! There's the historic fortified castle of the Chateau Fort De Lourdes being strategically placed at the entrance to the seven valleys of Lavedan. The town is surrounded by three smaller Pyrenean summits which are the Beout, the Petit Jer and the Grand Jer which reach up to nearly three thousand, three hundred feet. Southward from the town, the high peaks of Aneto, Montaigu, and Vignemale rise in all their splendour. The home for the orphaned children is a prominent building on the edge of the village and it appeared to be well maintained with its grounds including a large meadow area abloom with wild flowers and a mixed orchard of pears, apples and cherries.

We saw immediately a young lady in a wheelchair. With her was another young lady whose features mirrored the photo of Priscilla that Sir Martin had provided us with. As we watched, we saw a youth approach who spoke to them for a few minutes. As he was leaving, they all burst out into laughter. We approached the ladies and greeted them with good humour and asked if we could have a look at their paintings.

They were both painting a picture depicting the orchard and wild flowers with the distant hills in the background. The painting of the girl in the wheelchair was outstanding in its quality. The detail in the blossom and wild flowers was so fine that it made the painting very much alive. The painting of the other girl was very good but nowhere near the same quality. Both young ladies gave us a welcoming smile. Bigsby was the first to speak.

"What beautiful paintings, and to my mind more beautiful than the Old Masters. The flowers are so real it feels as though I can pick them. It must be a very enjoyable and rewarding hobby and one that I'd love to try."

"My friend is the artist who has natural talent as you can clearly see," said the girl they believed to be Priscilla. "My main interest is music in which I am at present writing a thesis for my doctorate. I was born into an artistic household where both my parents were well known artists, but even with their tuition I'd have been unable to have reached the stature of a professional. I do enjoy painting here with the spectacular mountain scenery as a backdrop."

"You must be Priscilla," said Bigsby. "Your parents are so worried about you. We're friends of your mother and she's asked us to help find you as she's very concerned about your welfare. My name is Lord Bigsby and this is my friend, Field Marshal James. Our French colleague and friend is General Couture. For your mother's sake, would you please come back to London with us tomorrow?"

"Oh my! I had no idea!" replied Priscilla. "I know my mother must be worried about my whereabouts and I'm sorry that I didn't inform her. You see, she thinks my father was murdered, and worries that I may be a target too. But my father was so honest and caring and here, especially, he was well respected by all."

I then asked the young woman in the wheel chair about her life at Lourdes.

"There's nothing else to do here for me but paint. I've always longed to climb the mountains and see the birds that inhabit the heights. To behold the Alpine Accentor, the Snow Finch and the Black Woodpecker would have been magic for me. The Golden Eagle and the Black Shouldered Kite I've longed to watch in flight while standing on the mountain tops."

They all spoke together for a while. The young woman in the chair said, "As you know, my friend's name is Priscilla. My name is Carolee. We first met in unusual circumstances over two years ago and became friends. Priscilla has been with me for about four weeks now and we've become like sisters. Her father, Lord Percy, always visited me when he was in the area and was so kind and understanding towards me. We're really friendly, carefree young ladies with no enemies, I assure you, but loads of friends. Our passions are in the artistic field and we're both lovers of classical music, especially the music of the revered French composers Chopin and Debussy. Our favourite pieces are Chopin's Polonaise in A-Flat Major Opus 53 and Claire De Lune by Debussy. There's a talented classical pianist in the town which we often have the pleasure of listening to. We both play the piano when an opportunity arises, but Priscilla could become a well-known performer in her own right. I'm sure she will give you a rendition of Mozart's Piano Concerto in C Minor on her return home. It will transport you into another world."

I then asked who the young man was who'd spoken to them earlier.

"His name is Dax and he befriended me nearly three years ago," said Carolee. He's so kind to me and understanding of my infirmity and often takes me out in my wheelchair to enable me to paint different views of the landscapes. He's so much fun and often comes here to joke with us."

Bigsby then spoke with great emphasis.

"Ladies, it's urgent that you both come with us immediately. I'm an expert in the use of guns and I saw that the young man who spoke to you was armed. The gun was hidden in a shoulder holster and I immediately recognized this. I believe you should get your belongings and come with us at once. You may stay at our hotel before we travel back to London. General Couture will explain to the manager of the home about your absence."

"I can't come today," said Carolee, "but I'll come with you early tomorrow. I have an appointment which has been pre-planned for some time. My friend Dax often carries a gun so I assure you I will come to no harm."

Bigsby did all he could to persuade Carolee to come, but to no avail, although she did promise to be ready to go with us at ten o'clock the following morning.

Forty minutes later, we were on our way to Champs with Priscilla. On our arrival, the owner of Champs willingly made a room available for her and promised that he'd see that she was safe and that her food and requirements would be taken up to her room. Bigsby and I relaxed with a glass of port each while examining the menu for our fully deserved evening meal. Bigsby was the first to speak.

"It appears strange that the young ladies' friend Dax should be armed in such a quiet and peaceful place as Lourdes. It disturbs me greatly. What do you think we should do now?" Bigsby asked.

I told Bigsby that we should first enjoy our meal and reminisce with Couture about old times, as this would relax our minds and put the happenings of the day in a better perspective. There was no question but that he'd agree to this!

And what a meal it was—and it most certainly revived our spirits! Now it was time to relate to Bigsby what I thought our next course of action should be.

"I consider it most important, my friend, that we should speak to Priscilla tonight. So let's go up to her room and ask if this would be convenient."

We went upstairs immediately and gave a light tap on the door. She bade us come in. Priscilla was a very beautiful girl with striking features. Her sophistication gave her a beauty that set her apart. She moved with elegance and her delicate features gave her a calmness. Dressed in a pink blouse and floral skirt, she looked stunning.

Bigsby asked Priscilla if we could speak with her. After we were settled, he motioned to me to start the questioning.

"Why did you come to Lourdes, Priscilla, without telling your parents?" I asked quietly.

"No one knows how much I miss the love and affection of my father. I needed time away from home to gather my thoughts, and Lourdes, as my father loved the place so much, seemed the perfect place for me to come. I went to see Carolee as soon as I arrived and she was very willing for me to stay with her. I did mention to my mother a few weeks ago about coming here. I'm surprised she didn't mention this."

"I know how much you must miss your father, Priscilla. Your mother has asked us to investigate his death to see if there could be any suspicious circumstances in connection with it as she's not convinced he died of natural causes. Could you kindly answer a few questions for us in relation to this?"

"Certainly, Field Marshal James, as I agree with my mother that his death was suspicious."

"Was there anything at all that even slightly aroused your curiosity during your one week stay with your father in Lourdes?"

"He was very surprised but delighted to see me as I had come over without invitation. Willingly, he introduced me to Carolee and we formed a close bond almost immediately and we now look upon each other as sisters. My late father's and Carolee's talent for recreating landscapes on canvas is sheer genius and I took it for granted that this was how their friendship began as my late father mentioned to me how greatly her work had improved with his tutoring. I cannot think of anything that happened out of the ordinary during that time."

"Where did your father go to paint on the final day you were there and please try to bring to mind all that took place that day?"

"I recall that my father set off early that morning to allow himself time to reach a place where he told us that he hadn't painted from before. He'd found a path earlier that week, he informed us, that he hadn't known existed and he'd followed this path which he said brought him out to a most glorious vista, the likes of which he'd never before had the delight to experience.

"I was waiting for him on his return when I noticed two men running urgently towards him from behind of which he appeared unaware. One of the men tripped before he reached my father and the other man then gave up the chase. I haven't mentioned this to anyone before, but the men looked as though they were desperate to obtain something from him. This event had completely slipped my memory until now.

"My father was late returning, and thirty minutes later, we had to begin our journey home. I only saw the painting he did when we returned home and I judged it as the finest he has ever painted. It was a view of the Pyrenees I hadn't seen in any of his previous paintings.

"In the foreground, he included a strange-looking hut with the faces of two men at the window. One of the men at the window he painted as having red hair. There were also two other men outside the hut carrying things that resembled spades. It was superb and full of life, but amazingly had a somber feel about it. My late father gave it the title of, 'The Pyrenees and The Strange Hut'."

"Thank you very much for this information; it could be of vital importance. Finally, I'd like to know if your father left the house between the time he returned home and his death."

"On his return home, my father spent most of his time touching up the six paintings he'd completed on that particular trip and once they were dry, he framed them. It was usually between three and four weeks before he was happy with them and it was his usual custom then to take them personally to the internationally recognized high-class auctioneers of Peregrino's, as he did also on this occasion."

Bigsby asked if he might ask her a more personal question and she told him in no way would she be offended.

"Priscilla, what would you say if I suggested that Carolee come to live with you on a more or less permanent basis? This would give her a family life she's never experienced and also a place she could call home. Your mother would have to agree to this, of course."

"Oh my! I'd be delighted beyond words! Do you think this could be arranged, Lord Bigsby? I do hope so because Carolee and I have bonded with a real sisterly love. I find it very difficult to make friends. My interests, as those of Carolee, are confined to the arts and we would complement each other in so many ways."

"I'll ask Carolee if she is like-minded and, if so, I'll have a word with your mother about the matter. I may not look like a fatherly figure but I regard a good family life, with a real love for each other, of paramount importance. This will give you both a solid foundation to start your chosen path in life and I'm sure this could be—with your mother's help—for both of you."

"You've made my day, Lord Bigsby! It will also be a real help to me in overcoming my sorrow over the death of my father!"

I thanked Priscilla for her help in providing so much significant information.

The next morning, we went to Lourdes where we hoped Carolee would be waiting for us. We need not have worried as she came, without question, to Champs.

We helped her up to the room that she would be sharing with Priscilla and the two young ladies exchanged greetings. We then asked Carolee, a very attractive-looking young lady but who didn't possess the same grace as did Priscilla, if she would come into an adjacent room and answer a few questions we would like to ask her. She agreed.

"You told us that Lord Percy often visited you at the orphanage at Lourdes. Was it to help you progress as an artist?" asked Bigsby.

"He did help me with my paintings by advising what palette I should use. His use of colour was outstanding. Lord Percy visited me three times a year and has done so since I was born. He was very kind to me and without him, my life would have been unbearable."

"Why did he visit you so often, Carolee? How was it that he's known you all your life?"

"According to Lord Percy, I was born about the same time and in the same hospital as Priscilla and that both my parents deserted me at birth as they didn't want a disabled child. He told me that he offered to care for me and that he'd been advised to take me to the orphanage at Lourdes. Here I would receive the best care possible as well as be able to enjoy the warm, clear air of the area. He really has been very good to me."

"Do you know who your real parents are, Carolee?" I asked.

"I don't know and I don't want to know because of what they did to me."

"I'm so sorry this has happened to you," I responded. "I have great respect for Lady Helen who I regard as a person of high moral standing. How would you feel about living with Priscilla's family? I know Priscilla would be delighted."

"How wonderful that would be! I've missed a family life so much!. To have someone to confide in and to feel the warmth and understanding of a family around me and to have a sister who I love dearly would far surpass anything I've ever imagined. I'm in no way bitter about what took place as I've had a happy life and been well cared for, but many times I have felt so alone."

"I'll have a word with Lady Helen as soon as we return and I'll also have a word with a friend who I met at Oxford while studying and is now a world renowned specialist in paralysis to see if he can help you can gain movement in your legs. That's all for now, Carolee. You can return to your room. I need to have a word with Field Marshal James, and then we'll let you and Priscilla know of our next intention."

Bigsby may have his shortcomings but one cannot fault the importance he places on family life and love and affection within the family. Even in his army days, he always ensured that he spent ample time with his wife and two children to give them a stable and a loving upbringing.

CHAPTER FOUR

After we had discussed everything we knew about the case so far, I suggested to Bigsby that we should leave for home the following morning. He agreed with me that he should discuss with Lady Helen about the care of the young ladies while I made further enquiries into the painting that Lord Percy painted on the final day of his stay at Lourdes.

We had not yet decided on the importance of trying to establish who were the real parents of Carolee or if she was, in fact, telling the truth. The fact that she assured us that Lord Percy had committed himself to taking care of her we would keep in mind. We then informed the young ladies of our plans and then retired to bed in anticipation of an early start the following morning.

We said our farewells to Couture but we were all under the impression that we would be meeting again in a few days. We decided that on our return to London, we would ask Lady Helen's permission to consult Lord Percy's doctor. This would give us an indication as to any possibility that he had been killed.

We arrived back in London the following day where we saw the two young ladies safely settled in the home of Lady Helen.

"Lunch at The Club now, James, and we thoroughly deserve it." While lunching, Bigsby asked me what my plans were. I told him my first assignment after lunch would be to go to the offices of the Peregrino International Auction Services and enquire about Lord Percy's painting. Sir Martin was now working there and had become a senior executive. When he had first come to see us, we had been very doubtful of his character and his reasons for marrying Lady Helen. Now that we realized he had achieved so much success in his studies at Oxford, we were beginning to look at him in a different light.

His rise to Executive Director had been rapid and he was becoming well known in his sphere of work. On our first meeting with Lady Helen and Sir Martin, we had noticed how evident their love and affection appeared to be for each other, and their class difference didn't appear to worry either of them in the slightest.

This bemused us as on our initial acquaintance with Sir Martin, he gave both Bigsby and me the impression that he was totally apathetic toward both his wife and Priscilla. So it would be with Sir Martin that my enquiries would begin.

After lunch, Bigsby set off to see Lady Helen about the welfare of the young ladies. I set off to the Peregrino Auction House to make an appointment with Sir Martin. Fortunately, Sir Martin was available to see me immediately. I updated him on our progress so far and told him how we had found Priscilla safe and well. He appeared delighted beyond words.

"How wonderful to have my daughter back and I cannot thank you enough. I will support my wife if she thinks it best that this Carolee stays with us. Priscilla has few friends and for her to have a sister whom she could confide in would help her progress so much. She's a talented musician and I'm going to suggest to her that she join the London Symphony Orchestra to showcase her talent. Carolee will have no problem in exhibiting her art work at any of the prestigious venues."

"I would like information, Sir Martin, about the whereabouts of the painting, 'The Pyrenees and the Strange Hut'. This was Lord Percy's final painting before his death. He brought it here for auction the day before his death and it's of the utmost importance that, if it's been sold, we know who bought it and the circumstances surrounding the sale."

"As you will be well aware, it's not permitted for us to disclose details of the buyer apart from where there are exceptional circumstances. However, I do regard this as the case and, as a director, I now have the authority to provide you with all the relevant details. It will take me a couple of hours to do this and, if you are willing, it would be better if you could visit me at home as we'll have more freedom to talk there without the fear of being overheard."

"That's a splendid idea, Sir Martin. Bigsby and I will look forward to seeing you about eight o'clock this evening at your home."

When we arrived at Lady Helen's and Sir Martin's home, we received an exceptionally warm welcome. Lady Helen had agreed on letting Carolee live with them and there was much singing, piano playing and general joviality. Carolee thanked Bigsby warmly for his help to enable her to start the family life she'd never before experienced. Eventually, the ladies adjourned to another room and we were at last free to discuss the subject of Lord Percy's final painting. Sir Martin was the first to speak.

"An international auction specializing in fine arts was held approximately three weeks after Lord Percy submitted his latest works from the Pyrenees. From our records, he submitted six paintings which included the one entitled, 'Pyrenees and the Strange Hut'. His other five art works sold quickly within the auction's estimated valuation.

"This one painting sold at nearly double the auction valuation and we, at the auction house, looked at this as suspicious as it was the only bid. Nearly always, the bids would start at a much lower price and increase accordingly. The buyer was present and he paid in cash which was even more surprising.

"Our Auction House always keeps a copy of the record for each painting that enters our saleroom but on this occasion, I've been unable to locate it. The payment clerk wrote a note on the file to say he was sure that the purchaser had a Spanish look about him.

"That's all I've been able to find out and I do hope it helps with your enquiry. Thank you again, Lord Bigsby, for your help in bringing Carolee into our family and we will care for her dearly as we do for Priscilla."

We both thanked him for all this information and then spent an hour chatting and singing with the happy family. Before leaving, we asked Lady Helen if she would give us permission to visit Lord Percy's doctor so that we could discuss with him the uncertainty he had about the cause of his death. She willingly agreed and told us that she would contact the doctor and let us know when he was available to see us. We then said our goodbyes.

When I arrived at the office the next day, Bigsby was already there sitting in a pensive mood. I decided to cheer him up with a joke. "Did you hear, my Lord, that O'Gara was arrested for armed bank robbery. When the jury found him not guilty, O'Gara said that was great and did it mean he could keep the stolen money? Ha."

"Not now, James. I've been thinking."

I was in total shock! Never before in the many years I'd known him had I ever heard him say that he'd been thinking! It made me realize that his emotional involvement in finding the real cause of death of Lord Percy for the sake of Lady Helen's family must be immense.

"James, have we ever considered why Lord Percy took Carolee to an orphanage at Lourdes a few days after she was born? Were there not many other orphanages where it would have been easier to take her? Why did her parents flee immediately after her birth? Maybe it was true that they didn't want a disabled child, but surely all parents would love their children, whatever their state of health, when born."

"Are we not better, Bigsby, to keep an open mind for the moment?"

At eleven o'clock, we received a message from Lady Helen to say that the doctor would see us at his surgery at two o'clock that afternoon.

"Before we visit the doctor, Bigsby, I'd like a few minutes chat with Lady Helen and then a visit to the Mayfair Memorial Hospital where Priscilla and Carolee were born."

This was agreed upon and also that I would meet Bigsby back at the office at one o'clock. Lady Helen and the ladies were pleased to see me. I asked Lady Helen if Lord Percy's style of painting had altered after his first visit to the Pyrenees.

"His style of painting did not change as this was a style peculiar unto himself. What did change was that he became more absorbed in his work and he spent more hours than I would have wished standing by his easel painting. Previously, his artwork had been what I would have called a serious but enjoyable hobby while earning more than adequate for our needs with his investments.

"He always made sure we were well cared for and that we were able to take adequate trips to the countryside where we were all immensely happy. After Priscilla was born, he became known as a prodigious landscape artist but also one of remarkable talent, where many likened his skill to that of Constable."

I assured her that we would keep in touch and then walked slowly to the hospital in Mayfair. I explained to the sister in charge why I'd come and after consulting the records, she informed me that the matron who was on duty at that time, and was assisting with the births, was away on holiday in the USA but would be back on duty in a few days. I thanked her and told her I'd return and then walked back to the office deep in thought.

It took Bigsby and me only thirty minutes to walk to the doctor's home where he held his surgery. It was a large semi-detached house of Tudor design in a pleasant middle-class area of London.

The doctor must have been waiting for us as he answered the door immediately. We were ushered into his surgery where the medical files of Lord Percy were already open on a large mahogany table.

"Lord Bigsby and Field Marshal James, I presume. I understand you require information regarding the death of Lord Percy. My name is Dr.

Staywell and I've been the doctor for the Fairdown family for forty years, so I know them well."

"Very pleased to meet you, Dr. Staywell," replied Bigsby. We'd like to know if his death was in any way suspicious or if it was clearly from natural causes."

"A very difficult question and one which I cannot truthfully answer. My first thought when I saw him was that it was a suspicious death, as though he'd suffered a fit. Knowing Lord Percy as I did and the great respect he was held in, I could think of no one who would want to kill him. After consulting my colleague, I decided to put his death down to natural causes with a proviso that there was uncertainty."

"How would you sum up your thoughts, Dr. Staywell?" I asked.

"To put it simply, I consider that there's a strong possibility that he could have been killed, but on the other hand, his death could have been from natural causes. I would say that looking into his death as a possible murder may not be a waste of your time. I have here my official record of cause of death with the proviso attached, which you can keep. I must now bid you good-day as my first patient will be arriving shortly."

"Very non-committal I'd say, James, but he did give the impression that he thought there was a strong possibility of murder."

"Let's concentrate for the moment in investigating his death as suspicious and see where that leads us, Bigsby."

Priscilla told us that Lord Percy was painting in a remote spot on his last day at Lourdes, which he had always considered to be inaccessible. Maybe he had accidentally discovered something that ultimately led to his death. It could easily be connected to the strange hut and the men he included in his painting—the one that Priscilla described to us."

"I will follow your advice, James, but do let us be extra careful and thorough in our investigation."

"Let's first visit The Hut and see if there's anything that arouses our suspicion. Could you make arrangements for our return to Champs and our accommodation there? Also, ask the manager if he would be able to obtain a map of the area to enable us to find the way to The Hut."

Couture was not able to meet up with us for twenty four hours because of a prior engagement ,but he'd made certain that the owner of Champs would provide us with a large scale map. On arrival, the hotelier said how pleased he was to see us again and handed us the map. We retired upstairs to our rooms to examine it in privacy. Imagine our excitement when we saw a building marked thereon in the area where Lord Percy had been painting. Looking at the contours of the map, it did seem impossible to get to, but we knew there must be a way.

After another specialty dinner from the Champs menu and a bottle of wine produced from their own vineyard, we discussed our plans for the following day. We decided, finally, that our priority was to find a way to access The Hut in the mountains and, if no one was about, to take a look inside.

"Well, James, old boy, I'm not going there without my old trusty Walther and you'd better take that huki kuri thing the Gurkhas gave you. Who knows, someone may be waiting to kill us so we'd better be extra cautious."

Wise words indeed from Bigsby. After breakfast, we travelled to Lourdes and made the Orphanage our starting point. We'd seen from the map that if we made the mountain of Pic Du Midi our guiding point for the first mile, we would be very near the hidden path to The Hut which we then would have to locate.

I asked Bigsby if he had any desire to climb the mountain, but at 9,439 feet, he said he had none, but in a much more impolite way!

"Did you know, Bigsby, that astronomers have been climbing the Pic Du Midi since 1884. The views from the summit extend across the whole of the Pyrenees range and even further afield. Because of the excellent viewing conditions, it was decided in 1878 to build an observatory at the top of the mountain. When completed in 1908, the eight meter dome housed a powerful mechanical equatorial reflector. I'm sure I've now persuaded you to trek to the summit with me as I can see the uncontrolled excitement on your face!"

"Building an equatorial reflector on a mountain over three thousand miles from the equator! You're having me on, James!"

Once on our way, we spent a lot of time just looking for the path indicated on the map. After two hours of searching, we suddenly found the tiny path. For the first few yards, someone must have strewn boulders to make it appear there was no access. From here, we could clearly see The Hut in a hollow on the hillside. The climb to it tested our fitness but we eventually arrived there although much out of breath.

It appeared to be an old, stone-built, shepherd's hut that was no longer used and had fallen into disrepair. With the sheep and lambs wandering the hillside, it was easy to imagine a shepherd and his wife living here with their collies. The slopes were ablaze with the yellow of the broom while cowslips, marguerites, wild anemones and gentians grew in abundance.

"Cor blimey, James! Look at all those chains and padlocks and the shutters on the windows. It reminds me of a miniature Colditz! Something fishy is going on here."

"Looks like someone left hastily, my Lord. The door's been left open and the chains and padlocks are all thrown to one side. I don't think they will have left anything behind, but maybe there may be a small clue somewhere."

Carefully, we entered the hut. On the floor, we saw bodies.

"Not left anything behind did you say, James? Blooming heck! Damn and Blast! Two dead men! I'm going to make sure my Walther's handy."

"We'll have to maintain our concentration now and keep our eyes peeled for the slightest movement," I said, as we moved back outside. "Wait a minute, Bigsby! Look!" I pointed to a man disappearing over a hill. "That's the friend of Carolee who was speaking to her at the orphanage. Thank goodness you saw that gun he had and we took Priscilla back to Champs."

"I'm going to ask the police for a guard at Lady Helen's house and forbid any of them to leave, even Sir Martin. I'll have their food and necessities taken to them by a trusted friend. Looking at these killings, James, they're not the work of a professional killer, but deadly effective none the less. A professional killer would know where to aim to kill immediately, but here they shot them randomly."

"Is this coincidence, James, or do you think there is any connection with Lord Percy?"

"Too early to come to any conclusion yet, Bigsby. We'll have to get back and inform Couture. Hopefully, he'll be waiting for us at Lourdes. After the scientific team has done their jobs and removed the bodies, we'll return and see if we can detect anything ourselves, however minuscule."

"Have you any thoughts yet why Lord Percy chose the orphanage at Lourdes, James?"

"Lourdes is a place of pilgrimage. It's where Bernadette Soubirous, who was a peasant girl, said she saw the Virgin Mary eighteen times in 1858. But that's no reason for him choosing Lourdes. Well, let's get back now, Bigsby, and tell Couture about the bodies and see what he advises."

General Couture was waiting for us, as previously arranged, and we updated him on the case so far. He immediately contacted the Police Department who sent officers with all haste to Lourdes. Two officers from the forensic department and four more officers to assist in the removal of the bodies soon arrived. Their job was to make a general examination of The Hut and its surroundings. We gave them detailed directions on how to get there and they set off without delay.

After talking matters over with Couture, we decided to return to London the following morning to await developments.

As the time was getting late, we returned to Champs for our evening meal which we were sure would sustain us until we reached London. Couture promised to keep in touch, so early the next morning we started on our journey back to London. We had boarded the ferry to Southampton before I realized how dumb I had been.

"As there's so much uncertainty about Lord Percy's death, isn't it obvious that a post mortem should be carried out? This will mean exhumation of the body but I'm sure Lady Helen will agree to this. We need definite proof whether Lord Percy died under suspicious circumstances. As soon as we arrive in London we will pay her a visit."

"A great idea, James. It appears strange that Dr. Staywell didn't advise a post mortem, but ours is not to reason why."

CHAPTER FIVE

We were both missing our families and so we decided to spend a few hours with them and then meet in our office at The Club. I knew Bigsby would be eager to check on any new cases of wine that had been delivered and, of course, sample them. He always assured me that spirits kept one's mind active, but I was a bit dubious about this as often I'd hear snoring coming from the direction where he was seated after an hour of sampling!

When we met we felt refreshed after having spent a few hours with our minds distracted from the case. It was now time for us to visit Lady Helen.

We made our way there and the family was all so pleased to see us. Priscilla was playing a Mozart composition on the piano while Carolee was humming to the tune as she painted. They all looked so contented and happy, but inside I'm sure they were all still worried about the death of Lord Percy who seemed to have been such a peace loving man.

We asked Lady Helen if we could speak with her alone

"Certainly, Bigsby and James. Come into the dining room where we will be alone."

After speaking with her about the need for an exhumation and post mortem, she was in total agreement.

"Certainly, I will agree. Just knowing what happened to Percy will ease my mind enormously."

"If you're willing, Lady Helen, we will go to the Ministry of Justice immediately to obtain a license for permission to exhume the body. I have a good contact who has a senior position in the Ministry so I don't expect any problem," said Bigsby.

To save time, we took a cab to the Ministry where Bigsby's acquaintance took us into his office.

"What brings you here, Bigsby, my friend? I've thought many times about visiting you at The Club, so maybe one day soon I will."

Bigsby explained our reason for coming and handed him the letter that Dr. Staywell had given us which stated his conclusions on Lord Percy's death.

"There does seem enough doubt both in the doctor's mind and in Lady Helen's also to issue you a license for exhumation. I'll arrange for this to be done tomorrow."

We thanked him for his kindness before heading for the Coroner's office in Horseferry Road. It was only a short stroll over the bridge across the River Thames. It was a beautiful day and we stopped for a few moments to watch the graceful swans gliding majestically on the river. I tried to picture the horse ferry that crossed the river with its passengers before the bridge was built.

The Coroner was very helpful after we explained to him our purpose for coming. He asked to see our license for exhumation. After consulting his papers, he said a post mortem could be done the day following the exhumation. As it was Lord Percy, he would obtain the services of Dr. Guttman who was considered the best forensic pathologist in London.

Everything had been very quickly arranged. A privilege of the aristocracy, according to Bigsby! We walked with Lady Helen back to her home before heading for our office. After a glass of wine at The Club, we decided to spend the next three days with our wives and children, now in their late teens, to await the outcome of the autopsy.

It was a great time of relaxation for us both. Bigsby took his two sons, both football fanatics, to watch Arsenal Football Club. Since the appointment of Herbert Chapman as their manager the team was now playing well. Bigsby, I'm sure, would have roared the team on as much as the boys. I took my two daughters to Wimbledon for a game of tennis where I was easily defeated by them both!

After a really enjoyable few days, it was back to our office where the result of the autopsy was expected later that day. We had both been invited, along with Lady Helen, to attend the surgery of Dr. Guttman at three o'clock. When we arrived, Lady Helen was already in the waiting room. She appeared tense and anxious.

Half an hour later, the doctor called us into his surgery before he spoke in gentle tones to Lady Helen.

"Lady Helen, I have examined the organs and tissues and done an evaluation of the body fluids. I'm sorry to tell you that there's no doubt at all that Lord Percy died of strychnine poisoning."

Lady Helen immediately started to cry but soon recovered. She now knew how her husband had died and it was up to us to find the killer. We walked with her back to her home where she was immediately comforted by Priscilla. We said we'd return the next day to discuss matters with her. We then went back to our office.

"What next I hear you ask," said Bigsby.

"Correct, James, but first of all I'd like to know the effect of strychnine poisoning on someone."

"Strychnine affects the central nervous system, Bigsby. It causes severe convulsions while the victim is still conscious with death usually occurring due to respiratory failure."

"Well, what happens next? If it's Lady Helen's wish for us to continue our investigation, I suggest we first of all speak to Priscilla and Carolee. We'll try and jog their memories about anything they saw regarding Lord Percy which they'd consider unusual.

"Secondly, I suggest that, with Lady Helen's permission, we go to Lord Percy's bank and enquire about his finances since Priscilla was born. I would assume that he banked with the London Nobility Bank but Lady Helen can confirm this.

"Thirdly, it may now be a good idea if we're able to search the records of all births that took place around the time that Priscilla and Carolee were born. This may enable us to find out who Carolee's real parents are.

"At least it will keep us busy for a couple of days and hopefully uncover a few more clues for us to work on. What do you think, Bigsby?"

"I think we deserve a meal at The Club tonight, James. Let's go and see what's on the menu."

We both decided on pork loin with apricot sauce. The pork was from the Gloucester Old Spot breed of pig and was deliciously juicy and fresh.

"Well, Bigsby, what do you call a pig that does karate? A pork chop! Ha!"

We visited Lady Helen again the next morning to find out if she wished us to continue our investigation.

"Yes, I'd like you to carry on where you left off at Lourdes. It may be coincidence that Percy included The Hut in his final painting, nevertheless,

I feel there is a connection. Call it woman's intuition but I'm sure the trail will lead you to the killers of Percy."

I then asked the girls if they could remember anything unusual.

"Can either of you recall anything at all that you considered highly unusual at any time, or noticed that Lord Percy's actions were different to what you might have expected? Carolee, were you aware of what happened to the two paintings he took to Lourdes each time he went to see you? Are you aware of what he did on the days he didn't paint?"

"The paintings were undoubtedly the work of Lord Percy," Carolee said. "They were collected from him by one of the local dignitaries of the area, as far as we were told. They always appeared very amiable towards each other and the dignitary always thanked him profusely. I knew the man as Guy but he only visited the Orphanage on the days that Lord Percy arrived.

"Each week Lord Percy would spend three nights away from Lourdes but he didn't say for what reason, nor did I ask as it would have been very impolite of me."

I then asked Priscilla if she could add any more information.

"On three occasions I noticed that he took two of his paintings to the Bank just prior to his visits to Lourdes when he told us he was going to deposit them with the Peregrino Auction House. I was having coffee in the café across the street and he didn't see me. After about thirty minutes he came out of the bank still holding them and returned, back home. I'm not aware of anything else unusual in his actions."

We thanked them both and then headed to The London Nobility Bank. Lady Helen had written a letter for us to take to the Bank which gave them permission to help us in any way possible and allowed them to reveal to us any financial transactions of Lord Percy's which we thought essential to the case.

The Bank was situated on Lombard Street which had been a centre for banking and insurance stretching back to medieval times. We passed the sign for the old site of Lloyds' Coffee House and looking up, saw the splendid Golden Grasshopper sign with many other colourful ones depicting the sites of historical buildings. These were erected for the coronation of Edward VII. What I would have given for a view of the street then, with its commercial and financial activity!

Bigsby was well acquainted with the bank's manager, and they greeted each other with much aplomb. Sir Edward Noteworthy, as his name was, extracted the relevant files from their place of safe keeping before finding the financial accounts for the previous twenty-five years. Sir Edward spoke in what was now known as his trademark staccato voice.

"Most of Lord Percy's business investments were passed down to him by his father, Lord Harry. Lord Harry was a very astute businessman according to my father, but my father did mention also that he lost a lot of money on one unfortunate enterprise. This was due, he told me, to a very unexpected and severe downfall in the financial markets which unstabilized the economy, but with Lord Harry's immense fortune, he was able to ride the storm and he soon made back his money by investing more in the property market.

"What happened to the other person involved in the enterprise, he didn't know, but he said unless he had substantial funds it would most likely have made him bankrupt. Apart from the sudden downturn in the economy, my father believed both sides would have made a considerable profit.

"Lord Percy had a large property portfolio in the wealthy Cashmere area of London, which included large houses, jewelry shops, ladies and gents outfitters for the aristocracy, as well as a number of other high class businesses. He also owned four properties in Sussex, where the family enjoyed spending a few days holiday on the coast near Brighton. The interest created from this portfolio was of such proportion as to keep the family in real luxury. The total value of his properties must run into millions.

"Twenty years ago on the sixth of April, Lord Percy withdrew, in cash, the large sum of twenty thousand pounds. I remember clearly questioning him about withdrawing such a large amount but he assured me that all was fine and the money was required for a purely personal reason. I do have his signature here authorizing this.

"There have been a number of reasonably-sized payments into his account which are shown here as having come from the Peregrino Auction House which I presume to be the proceeds from his paintings. Three times a year he withdrew reasonably large amounts in cash and asked to be left alone in a private room to count it.

"Let us see now. Twelve years ago, he purchased a large estate in the Pyrenees—Campan Estate, which included a livestock farm with modern horse breeding facilities where many fine pedigree racehorses were reared. Many winners of major horse races were bred on the estate and there were two runners in the inaugural race of the Prix de L'Arc de Triomphe in 1920, which is France's most famous horse race, but I didn't hear of their placements.

"This was purchased with the money acquired from the sale of two of his substantial properties in Sussex; he retained the other two properties which continue to be used for their vacations.

"There were no suspicious circumstances in regard to the financial aspect of the sale as it was acquired through Taraya Estate Property Services in Barcelona, which is a sister company of Peregrino Auction House. Both of these companies have a reputation which is second to none.

"Lord Percy did confide in me that he'd become interested in something to do with racehorses while staying in Sussex on vacation and had become very close friends with Sir Clive Ponywood, who's a veterinary surgeon. Sir Clive specializes in the care of farm animals and is an authority in the treatment and breeding of thoroughbred racehorses of which he has expert knowledge.

"Up to two years before his death, it appeared that his purchase of this estate had been an excellent financial investment while at the same time allowed him to gain greater knowledge of his interest. During the last two years before his death, he received no income at all from his Campan Estate and the outgoings from the six months previous to that took nearly all the substantial profits accrued over the previous seven or so years. Lord Percy must have been a very worried man.

"The only possibility for this that I can think of is that he either sold the estate or was doing his transactions through another Bank. If he'd sold the

Estate, unless he was banking with another company, then the proceeds would surely have been paid in here.

"There must have been some changes that took place there which I'd advise you to investigate, but please, Lord Bigsby and Field Marshal James, be extremely vigilant. Possibly the large expenditure over that year could have been an upgrading of the estate or an expansion on the farm or possibly the purchase of more horses for breeding purposes as the best horses bring a huge price.

"The account relating to the estate was suspended on the death of Lord Percy and we were hoping soon to find out who the legal owner of the estate should now be unless, of course, he sold it without our knowledge. He also withdrew the sum of £5,000 nearly seven years ago and the payee paid this into the Banque de Marseilles in France.

"Winding up his affairs after his death has been a long and painstaking process which is not yet complete. That's all his financial details to date and I do hope I've been some help in your investigation. I'm unable to give you the name of the manager of the estate as this can only be obtained from Taraya Estate Properties in Barcelona and you'll also need written consent from the solicitor of Lady Helen."

"Thank you, Sir Edward, and I'm sure this information will be of extreme value and hopefully will lead us to the killer of Lord Percy. Please do come and join myself and James at The Club one day as I can assure you the food and wine are of exceptional quality."

We had certainly gained ample information which needed to be sorted out, but Bigsby insisted that we spent the rest of the day with our families once again as this would help to freshen our minds.

I was early in our office the next morning as I'd been trying to make sense of all the information we'd been given the previous day, and I'd been unable to sleep. I knew Bigsby would have slept well as during all the time I'd known him, he had relied on me to unravel all our difficulties and therefore it was easy for him to switch off as he knew I would bear all the responsibility. At last Bigsby arrived.

"What are our plans for today, James, my boy? I had a really good sleep last night and I feel so much refreshed with having a few hours off from our case."

"I've been thinking, Bigsby, that the twenty thousand pounds withdrawn by Lord Percy on the sixth of April twenty years ago was only two or three days after the births of Priscilla and Carolee, and I wonder if there's any connection. Our first task will therefore be to go to the offices of the registrar to see what births were registered around the fourth of April.

"After that, it will be necessary to go to Lady Helen's solicitors to get the appropriate documents to allow us to gain access to the name of the manager of the Campan Estate from Taraya Estate Properties in Barcelona. As soon as we're able to do this it will then be important for us to return to Lourdes and assess the case with General Couture. I don't know yet if it'll be necessary to visit Sir Clive Ponywood to ascertain if he has any involvement in Lord Percy's property in France."

"The registrar, Sir Tony Newborne, is a great friend of mine, James; he's a connoisseur when it comes to food and wine, so I consider it a good idea to ask him to lunch at The Club. After two or three glasses of Burgundy, he may disclose more information than what he intended!

"After lunch, we'll go to the offices of Lady Helen's solicitors. If you'd like to go and get the address from her and a signed letter to allow the solicitor to disclose all relevant information to us, it would save time later. My urgent task is to go to see the chef here and arrange for him to put on a gourmet lunch for Sir Tony."

Bigsby and food! I made my way slowly to Lady Helen's, wondering about Bigsby's choice of lunch menu. She was more than willing to give her solicitor the authorization to disclose any information we thought was necessary to our enquiries. I stopped for thirty minutes chatting with Priscilla and Carolee who told me it was the happiest they'd been in their lives and how much they'd been helping and supporting each other. They pleaded with me to find Lord Percy's killer as soon as we could as this was a real worry to them.

I returned to The Club where Bigsby and Sir Tony were already perusing the menu and discussing the wine list with great interest. They eventually decided on chestnut and mushroom paté for starters and grilled lobster with shrimp and salmon for the main course, washed down with a bottle of chardonnay and a bottle of chenin blanc. I thought Bigsby was going over the top but he'd been wanting the chef to try this menu for some time. It did sound delicious and I was hoping we'd both be sober enough to meet with Lady Helen's solicitor later in the day. What a superb meal and Sir Tony was certainly in a very talkative mood when we retired to our office to find out what information he had to give us.

"Well, Bigsby and James, that indeed was one of the finest meals I've ever tasted. Now down to business. I have with me all the files relating to births in London for the fourth of April and the two days either side of it. On the day in question, there were four births recorded. One was at the Mayfair Memorial Hospital and three at the Oval Children's Hospital."

Bigsby motioned for me to reply. "It's the Mayfair Memorial Hospital we're interested in, Sir Tony. Was there a child born there who was christened with the name of Priscilla Fairdown? We are also interested in any other children born around this time and who their parents are."

"Well, let me look, James. Indeed there was. The daughter of Lord Percy, no less, and a beautiful child I heard she was. There was one other child born at the Mayfair Memorial Hospital one day previous to this who was disabled and abandoned by her parents immediately after the birth and she was christened Carolee Cheetah. I understand she was taken to an orphanage in Lourdes soon after her birth and has been very well cared for."

"Can you tell us anything about her parents, as this information may be of great importance."

"I know very little. The birth was registered in the name of Mrs. Cheetah. A note has been attached to the birth record indicating Cheetah may have been the mother's maiden name and the child was most probably born from an extramarital affair. Although there are a number of people with the surname of Cheetah, the police were unable to trace her. It is more than likely she abandoned the baby to escape the wrath of her husband. It's also possible that her husband spent a lot of time away from home and she became a little bored! The father wished to remain anonymous so you'll have to get a court order to obtain this."

We thanked Sir Tony for his help and the information he'd given us and he once again thanked us for such a gourmet meal. Bigsby and I had no time to discuss this information between ourselves as we were due to see Lady Helen's solicitor, Mr. Mark Lawson. We arrived at his office a few minutes before our scheduled time and he greeted us warmly and bade us go into his private office. He already had the file of Lord Percy on his desk.

"Please let me know what information you need and I'll willingly provide it for you. I believe you require information about the purchase of the Campan Equestrian and Agriculture Estate in the Pyrenees. I did have the pleasure of a visit to the estate about eight years ago. What a stunning place, with the plateau of Payolle and its picturesque lake so close by. It's very close also to the Col de Tourmalet where the Tour de France is run."

I replied, "We'd like to know any details you have regarding Lord Percy's purchase of the estate and we'd like authorization from you that allows the Taraya Estate Properties in Barcelona to bestow on us any details we consider appropriate to our enquiries into the death of Lord Percy."

"Yes, James, I can give you the authorization you require, but I have no connection at all with Lord Percy's purchase of the estate nor do I possess any details. I received personal correspondence from the Taraya Estate Properties shortly after the sale that it must be kept strictly confidential. If you're able to wait a few moments, I'll write out the necessary permission you need for your enquiries into matters regarding the estate."

We thanked Mr. Lawson for his help and proceeded back to our office to mull over all the information we'd received. Bigsby poured himself a glass of wine and went over to the mirror where he started to drink it. I was perplexed and asked him what he was up to.

"Well, James, I went to the doctor this morning and he told me I had to watch what I drank! Ha!"

"Very comical, my Lord, but how do you sum up our day?" I asked him.

"We have gained a lot of information and a visit to Barcelona does seem urgent."

"I couldn't agree more, Bigsby, so tomorrow we'll return to Lourdes to see what Couture and the French police have been able to uncover. It's important that we visit Barcelona as soon as possible."

CHAPTER SIX

The next day, we set off once more to Champs and I could see that Bigsby was deep in thought once again.

"I hope you've been reading up on your horse racing and ...."

"Drat, what a stupid idiot I am! Your mention of horses has brought it back. I met a person who trains horses for the nobility about twelve months ago and his name is Lord Furlong. The name stuck in my mind as I thought how apt it was for someone with an interest in racing. If I'd remembered earlier we could have made enquiries about Sir Clive while we were still in London. I'm sure Lord Furlong will know everyone connected with horse racing. He lives near the Goodwood Racecourse in Sussex. Maybe we can pay him a visit soon."

"Since we're now in France, we should continue with our investigations here and in Spain before returning to London, if you agree."

"I certainly do, James, and now that we're so close to Champs, I can feel very serious hunger pangs coming on!"

Couture was waiting for us at Champs and before our meal, he gave us a full account of how the investigations were going at his end. The police had made a full forensic examination of The Hut and had found nothing to arouse their suspicions apart from the two dead men. They had easily been identified as two small-time local criminals who may have been tempted into more serious offences by an offer of large amounts of cash by big time crime organizations. If this had been the case, they'd failed to realize that 'large amounts of cash,' meant they'd be killed when their usefulness was over. We thought it best to keep it to ourselves, for the moment anyway, that we knew they were friends of Carolee.

No other leads had been uncovered. We made Couture acquainted with our enquiries also and he said we'd have a discussion after our meal so we could all give our thoughts about what the next course of action should be. After another scrumptious meal, we settled down together in one of the private lounges.

"Well, James, you give your opinion of where we should go from here."

"I think, Bigsby, we should now be very careful as we don't know who or what we're up against. We do know they're not afraid to kill. My suggestion is that we should make for Barcelona tomorrow to obtain all the knowledge that's obtainable about the Campan Estate from Taraya Estate Properties. If everything goes well there, I think we should then go back to Lourdes to examine The Hut and its proximity very carefully, especially the surrounding area, in case any clues have been left behind."

After a little more discussion, it was agreed that Bigsby and I should travel to Barcelona, and Couture would make himself available in case of any emergency help we might need. We then retired to bed in anticipation of an early start the following day.

It was a glorious sunny day as we started for Barcelona. It was a magical experience as we crossed over the Pyrenees. Lord Percy had, without doubt, bought a property in one of the most scenic areas I've ever been. We were going with a little fear and trepidation as Barcelona was now known as 'la rosa de foc' or 'the rose of fire' and had become one of the most radical and bloody places in Europe. We saw the Arc de Triomf which is a triumphal arch and was built by the architect Josep Vilaseca i Casanovas as the main access gate for the 1888 Barcelona World Fair. When we arrived, we easily found the offices of Taraya Estate Services which was a palatial building in the middle of Barcelona.

We were greeted by a friendly young man by the name of Mr. Neric Taraya, who was the son of the owner, and had recently qualified as an estate agent.

"Welcome to Barcelona, Lord Bigsby and Field Marshal James. It's a pleasure to meet you both. Please tell me what information you require and I will gladly supply it, if at all possible. Lord Percy was a very valued and well esteemed client at our auction house in London."

I once again took the lead. "It's a pleasure to meet you also, Mr. Neric. I have here authorization from Lady Helen's solicitor to allow you to bestow upon us any details regarding the Campan Estate that we deem essential to our enquiries. Could you please let us know if Lord Percy was the sole owner and if there were any directors of the company? Also we'd like to know who the managers are and their home addresses and what business activities took place on the estate. In short, everything that you know."

"Please be seated while I bring you a bottle of red wine and a bottle of white wine from our local

Bodegas Torres Vineyard. I heard on the grapevine that you were both wine connoisseurs."

Bigsby's eyes lit up and his face became a picture of contentment when the wine arrived.

"Now down to business. According to our records, Lord Percy requested us to make enquiries about estates in the area which were suitable for both commercial farming and the rearing of thoroughbred racehorses.

"The Campan Estate had been on the market for only two weeks and appeared to us to be a business enterprise with much potential. We ourselves examined the accounts of the business and had a study done about the future viability of the commercial farming enterprise as well as obtaining a feasibility report about the possible start-up of a breeding centre for thoroughbred racehorses, by the well-established firm of Agropecuario Finca Sociedad from Madrid. On account of the first class reports we received back from this company and our own research, we advised Lord Percy to purchase the Estate."

Bigsby was sampling, or maybe drinking, the wine with eagerness and appeared to be blissfully unaware of the conversation, so I continued.

"Was Lord Percy the sole owner, Mr. Neric?"

"Yes, he was, but Sir Clive Ponywood, who was a veterinary surgeon, was Executive Director with sole responsibility for the horse-breeding and training side of the business. He was also overseer of the farming operations as Lord Percy only visited the estate for a few days a year. Sir Clive informed us that he was English and lived in Kent but furnished us with no firm address.

"There were two managers who were responsible for day to day operations and I'll give you their names and addresses before you leave. I did hear that they'd been replaced about two or three years ago but we thought it not necessary to enquire further. We've also been told that there has been major expansion, but we're not aware in what way. I'm afraid that's all the information I can provide you with at the moment."

"Thank you so much, Mr. Neric, and it does appear that Lord Bigsby is very impressed with the wine, and the vineyard will most likely be getting an order soon from The Club in London. We'll be trying to contact the previous managers soon and we will keep you informed as to our progress."

We made our way out of the offices with Bigsby a little wobbly on his feet and his speech slightly slurred.

"Please remember, James, the name of that wine producer as the two wines I tasted were of the finest vintage that I've ever tasted. I'll be advising The Club to purchase a few cases from here."

"Not the two bottles you *sampled*, my Lord, but the two bottles you *drank*. That wine producer was the offices of Taraya Estate Properties."

"Goodness, James, no! I must have been transported into another world by their quality. I do apologize."

As it was getting late in the day, we stayed the night in Barcelona. I related to Bigsby all that Mr. Neric had told us and we decided—or I decided—that we would first visit The Hut in the mountains for clues. Later, we'd attempt to locate the previous two managers of the Estate.

We then reminisced about our journey over the Pyrenees. I remembered from our school history lessons that Aneto was the highest mountain in the range at slightly over eleven thousand feet and was located in Aragon, Spain. We stopped to look at the tiered waterfall of Gavarnie Falls which is situated in the Cirque de Gavarnie at the head of the Gave de Pau river. At 1385 feet, it's the highest waterfall in mainland France. If I'd been Lord Percy, I would have spent much more time at Campan.

On our arrival back at Champs, Couture was waiting for us, but he had nothing further to add. Anyway, the next morning we began our walk to The Hut. It was a lot easier for us this time to find the hidden path and we made good time. Bigsby was still enthusing about the quality of the wine he'd tasted in Barcelona but I knew that this was his way of concentrating on the task ahead. We spent two hours examining every nook and cranny in The Hut but found nothing even to slightly arouse our suspicions. Then we went outside to see if there was anything there. About fifteen minutes later, I heard an excited voice.

"James, by gosh, look here! I'm certain this is a small trail of old blood by the look of the colour. Probably caught themselves on the rock over there."

"You've got mighty good eyes, Bigsby. Let's follow it down to that small dell. Heck look! The growth in that small area in the middle is noticeably smaller and the grass is much greener. It looks as though the ground here has been dug up sometime in the past. There's another slight trail of blood over there. Could it be that someone has been killed and then buried here?"

"If you're a marksman, James, you need good eyes, otherwise you'd never hit the bull. Let's get back and tell Couture so that he is able to get his experts to take a look."

It was late by the time we returned to Champs. Couture said he'd make sure his men investigated this the following morning and he was none too pleased that they hadn't noticed it when they'd searched earlier. Bigsby, somehow, persuaded Couture to buy us a bottle of champagne as we, with our little knowledge of detective work, had proved far more superior than the French police.

We set off to see if we could locate the two previous managers at the addresses given to us by Mr. Neric, at the same time as the police set off to examine the area around The Hut. We were soon able to locate the first house where a middle-aged lady opened the door and bade us to come in. We told her why we'd come and asked her if she'd give us details of the time her husband had been working at the Campan Estate and the reasons he'd left.

"Jacques started working at the estate just over twelve years ago now. He was thirty at the time and had always wanted to work with animals. We knew a Lord Percy from England had bought the Estate but it was Sir Clive Ponywood who asked dear Jacques and Pierre next door to be the Farm Managers as he'd heard of their interest in farming and that they were good and honest workers, which they were.

"They both loved their jobs and worked long hours because they regarded it as a hobby as well. For ten years, they worked hard and then slightly over two years ago, Jacques said their hours and pay had been reduced. They were told by Sir Clive that they were now forbidden to work or to enter the Campan Estate premises after five o'clock in the afternoon.

"Then one day, Pierre came round to ask Jacques if he would go back to Campan with him as he'd forgotten to give the cows their extra feed and as it was after five o'clock, he was a little afraid about going alone. Being very conscientious, they went back and we haven't heard from them since. We're still devastated, but the police won't do anything as the Estate claim they didn't enter the premises. If we just knew what had happened, it would be such a relief."

"Did either of them have red hair?" I asked

"Yes, Pierre had bright red hair and you could see him from miles away. They say people with red hair have bad tempers, but Pierre was such a lovely man, just like Jacques. Why? How did you know!?"

"I'm so sorry but I'm afraid I may have bad news for you. The police are at this moment searching an area where I think your husband and Pierre may have been last seen."

"If only we knew where and why. It's two years since they disappeared into thin air. It'll be heartbreaking, but a relief to know what has happened even if they're no longer alive."

"Did either of them give any indication that anything was wrong two years ago and why they were banned from entering the estate after five o'clock?"

"No, not in the slightest. They loved their work and it was a great shock."

We told her we'd keep her updated, as well as her neighbour, and made our way back to Champs to discuss our next move. Couture was already there waiting for us and looked very troubled and thoughtful.

"The police found two bodies in the disturbed ground that you described and they're as yet unidentified. The bodies are not believed to be those of Jacques and Pierre and, in any case, they both had dark hair. No-one else in the area has been reported missing during this long period but the police are still investigating. One appears to be of British nationality and the other of Spanish origin. They'd both been shot a number of times with one of them having severe bruising to his neck."

Bigsby was the first to respond. "If these four deaths are connected with Campan, as seems most likely, surely something illegal must be taking place. How do we find out without putting ourselves in severe danger?"

"I think it wise to get all the information we can before we consider a direct approach. If we do have to make a direct approach would you be able to assist us in any way, General Couture?"

"I'll give you all the assistance I possibly can, James, because I've been given the authority to do so."

"I'd like to go back to London tomorrow, my dear Lord, and visit the Peregrino Auction House. They had a number of paintings of Lord Percy's in store which the auction had been unable to sell because there was a possibility that there could have been recognizable people included in the paintings which could not be sold without their written permission. There's an off-chance that Lord Percy could have painted the person, who purports to be Clive Ponywood, in one of his paintings of the Goodwood racecourse while he was staying on holiday at Brighton."

CHAPTER SEVEN

We returned back to London the following day and, as usual, Bigsby's first thoughts were lunching at The Club where he would advise them about the possible purchase of a few cases of wine from the vineyard near Barcelona.

"I met someone last week, Bigsby, who said his non-alcoholic wine was delicious, but I told him he had no proof! Ha!"

After lunch, we made our way to the Peregrino Auction House where we were met by a colleague of Sir Martin. We advised him of our reason for coming and he took us into the store for us to examine the paintings of Lord Percy which contained people who could have been recognizable. Only three were of men and two were paintings of a racecourse. Could one of these men be Sir Clive Ponywood? After obtaining a copy of both paintings, we decided it was right that we should spend time with our families before visiting Goodwood.

The following day, we made our way to Goodwood Racecourse, near Chichester, in West Sussex. Situated high on the Downs with an Iron Age hill fort to the south and the cathedral city of Chichester below, the views are spectacular. Many consider that it's the most beautiful racecourse in the world. No wonder it's referred to as Glorious Goodwood.

Being slightly interested in horseracing while at Cambridge, I knew the first flat race had taken place here in 1802 on the estate of the third Duke of Richmond. When we arrived, we saw that we were in luck as this was the second day of a three day meeting.

It was very tempting to place a bet on one of the horses, but we were not gamblers. Many had lost money this way which had left them in debt and ruined their lives, so we were both very much against it.

As we walked around, Bigsby recognized one of the race-goers from his days at Oxford and, with a little name-dropping, we were escorted to the main grandstand and treated like royalty. At the close of the meeting, we were invited to an exceptional meal in the dining room where Bigsby was seated next to Lord Furlong. Half way through the meal, Bigsby broached the subject of Sir Clive Ponywood.

"As you may know, Field Marshal James and I have started a private detective agency for the upper class. Although, for confidential reasons I'm unable to go into detail, a person by the name of Sir Clive Ponywood has come to our attention during our investigation. Is it true that he's a veterinary surgeon with a special interest in racehorses?"

"Yes," replied Furlong, "Sir Clive is a veterinary surgeon and a real gentleman. He is, though, a very weak-willed person. Such weak-willed people of high repute are so open to blackmail these days as they're prepared to suffer wrong rather than to fight for their right. He has the reputation of being the leading authority on the treatment and breeding of racehorses. As far as we know, he still runs a horse breeding establishment in the south of France where he's doing very well in breeding potential champions with his horses being in very high demand."

"Thank you so much for all your hospitality, Lord Furlong. James and I hope to return one day to attend one of your meetings. By the way, was Lord Percy a member here?"

"Good gracious no! He had as much interest in horse-racing as I have in landscape painting. But maybe Sir Clive's passion and overwhelming enthusiasm for the sport rubbed off on him, as it does with most people.

"As far as we know, he no longer holidays in the area as we did hear a rumour, maybe about three years ago that he'd sold his remaining properties in Sussex for a huge amount and bought a vineyard in the south of France near the foothills of the Pyrenees. We don't know if this is true or not as everything was so hush-hush. The rumour was also going about that the sale of his properties in Norfolk and the purchase of his vineyard in France were being overseen by a small estate agent in Toulouse. Probably thought he had nothing to lose if he went there! Ha! Ha!"

"As you may have guessed," replied Bigsby, "we have been assigned in our role of private detectives to enquire about the death of Lord Percy which we now regard as murder. Is there anything else you're able to tell us about him which you think may help?"

"He was a very honest man and a brilliant landscape artist but if anyone got on the wrong side of him, he would make sure they received retribution, however long it took. This was the only flaw in his character that anyone noticed. I did know him slightly. The last time I spoke to him was in London a few months before his death when he said he'd arrived home from a business trip to France only a couple of hours previously and had visited Lourdes on his way back where he had got the shock of his life, but he didn't elaborate on this."

"Do you know who bought his properties in Sussex?" I asked.

"Yes, but they're personal friends of mine so I don't feel at liberty to say, although I can vouch for their honesty and integrity."

By this time, we'd finished our meal and had thanked them a second time for their help and hospitality. We did consider taking a look at the properties Lord Percy had just sold but as the new owners were of good repute, according to Lord Furlong, we decided there was no point. We then made our way back to London.

"'Curiouser and curiouser,' cried Alice, as Lewis Carroll wrote in *Alice in Wonderland*. It seems to be more like Bigsby and James in *Murderland*, my Lord!" I mused.

"Well, James, it certainly does get more curious and confusing all the time. At least we know now that Sir Clive has a good reputation but even people who have good reputations commit murder. The advantage these people have is that no one would ever suspect them. The possibility of visiting a vineyard, though, does make the case much more appealing.

"All that appears open to us now is to return to France and find ways to get more information about the goings-on at Campan. We'll have to use the utmost caution but I don't know as yet the best way forward in relation to this. Maybe Couture will have a suggestion as to what we should do. I think we should return tomorrow and see how events unfold."

"We also need to visit Toulouse to see if we can locate the estate agent who sold Lord Percy the vineyard and find out the name of it and where it's located. We can decide tomorrow which we do first, but I consider the latter to be more appealing as hopefully there will be no danger involved."

We returned to Champs the following day hoping that Couture had been able to make some progress in the case. We were both utterly baffled. Why had Lord Percy bought a vineyard when he already owned an agricultural estate in the Pyrenees? What reason could there possibly be? We had been told of his interest in horses but as to his interest in wine we knew nothing. Bigsby, of course, thought this was a possibility!

We had a thorough discussion after our meal and it was decided that the safest option at present was for myself and Bigsby to go to Toulouse the following day. Here we'd try and locate the estate agency that had dealt with Lord Percy's latest transactions. We were all agreed by the fact that Lord Percy had wanted no publicity that it would more than likely be one of the smaller agencies and that we would try these initially.

It had surprised us that the two bodies found near The Hut were not those of Jacques and Pierre, but we were thankful for their wives' sake that there was still hope for them even after so long. We had gathered a lot of data, but very little appeared to fit together.

"I'm so much looking forward to visiting Toulouse, my dear Bigsby. It's often referred to as 'la ville a rose' because of the purple-pink tint of its buildings. I remember from my studies at

Cambridge that its history goes back over 2,000 years which started with a small Celtic tribe settling in the Garonne valley.

"If you think we can spare one day off from our enquiries, I would love to explore the city. It would be a delight to cross over the old stone bridge of Le Pont Neuf and also to see the Canal du Midi which was built in the eighteenth century. As far as architecture is concerned, the Basilica of St. Sernin would be my choice as it's the largest surviving Romanesque church in Europe."

"Well, James, I do think we need a day off to recharge our batteries as the next few days will more than likely be difficult ones and could even be dangerous. We'll have to be alert all the time. We can visit the places you want as long as you include a trip to a vineyard, but not the one that was owned by Lord Percy, as we'll be going there soon enough and purely on business."

This was agreed and we had the most wonderful of days. To explore the unique architecture of an ancient city took me back to my student days while Bigsby purchased a bottle of shiraz and a bottle of merlot wine which had been recommended to him at the Chateau de Joie where the manor house dated from the mid-eighteenth century.

I made no comment to Bigsby about the vineyard owner being a good salesman as these were the two most expensive wines on display! I didn't want to spoil his day.

The following day, we were tramping the streets of Toulouse once again but we struck luck as we entered our third estate agent's office of the morning. After showing them our credentials and the letter from Lady Helen which gave them permission to disclose private information, the manager led us into a large room overlooking the main boulevard. He introduced himself as Monsieur Jean Monet and advised us that he was a distant cousin of the celebrated artist Claude Monet who, he said, was looked upon as one of the finest impressionist artists of his time. He asked politely how he could help us regarding Lord Percy and he looked very distressed to hear of his death. I motioned to Bigsby to speak first.

"Speaking about Claude Monet, sir, we are looking into the suspicious death of Lord Percy who was also a renowned landscape artist. We are private detectives who've been hired by Lady Helen to inquire into the death of her husband.

"During our investigations, we've been informed that Lord Percy bought a Chateau in this area which was financed by the sale of two of his substantial properties in Sussex, England. If you also have information regarding the Campan Estate he purchased just over twelve years ago, we'd be very grateful and it would be a great help in finding out if his death was indeed murder."

"I will indeed help you all I can, Lord Bigsby and Field Marshal James, but please call me Jean. In the short time I knew him I came to respect and admire Lord Percy greatly. All the three transactions were very complicated from a legal aspect. Eventually the contracts were finally authorized as legally binding and countersigned by a senior barrister in the city.

"The first transaction that took place was the sale of his properties in Sussex which, after the price was agreed, was reasonably straightforward apart from the clause where anonymity was required. This was eventually overcome. There were then ample finances available to cover the purchase of the vineyard.

Lord Percy retained the name of the vineyard which was the Chateau d'Amour or Chamour as it was lovingly referred to. The sticking point here was that the name of the proprietor had to be made public, but this was against Lord Percy's wishes. In the end, he donated one per cent of the property to myself so that I was able to register myself as part owner and this was sufficient by law, but highly unusual.

The business bank account with the Banque de Cologne is also in my name but there are safeguards in both instances, written into the contract, which identify Lord Percy and his heirs as rightful owners. I was bound by oath not to release his name but as Lord Percy is no longer alive, and it's a possible murder enquiry, I'm sure this no longer applies.

"The third transaction involved the sale of the Campan Estate, which was fully owned by Lord Percy, to Baron de Buena. The problem here was the agreement of a price between the two parties. Sir Clive Ponywood, who was the person negotiating the sale, was unyielding in his demand that the Baron would purchase the estate for only half its value and not a penny more. I was very surprised at this, as large agricultural estates were selling for considerably more than their value as they were considered a sound financial investment. Lord Percy seemed under intense pressure to accept the offer which, to my considerable shock, he did."

I then asked Jean if he'd heard of the death of Lord Percy before our arrival and also if he knew how Chamour was being managed.

"This is the first I've heard of his death and I'm so distressed at the passing away of such a lovely and genuine man. As regards Chamour, I know the managers have been worried about the non-appearance of Lord Percy as they have mentioned this to me on a couple of occasions during the last two months. I was actually in the process of sending out a confidential letter to the appropriate authority in London asking for information about his whereabouts, so I'm so glad you have come. If you require any more assistance please do let me know."

"We certainly will, Jean, and thank you for all you've told us as I'm sure this information will be of the utmost importance in helping us to uncover the reason for the death of Lord Percy."

Before we left, Jean gave us directions to Chamour and told us it was one of the most respected vineyards in the area which produced outstanding wines. Bigsby's face broke into a beaming smile at hearing this.

On the way back to Champs, we passed the town of St. Gaudens which took its name from the young shepherd, Gaudens, who was martyred by the Visigoths toward the end of the fifth century for refusing to renounce his faith. I was enjoying the ancient history of the area while Bigsby was on the lookout for vineyards.

We arrived back late, but not too late, for dinner. Couture had left a note to say he'd been called away but would be returning the following evening. We decided the next morning to visit Chamour which was situated about thirty miles south of Toulouse.

CHAPTER EIGHT

We set off the following morning in brilliant sunshine and the view of the Pyrenees was spectacular. Even Bigsby seemed keen on relocating here, being tempted by the weather, the scenery, and most of all, the vineyards. The vineyard was easy to find and it was situated in the most idyllic location. Lord Percy must have been super wealthy to afford a place like this.

The Chateau was built in the French Baroque style with its colonnades and cupulos. One could have mistaken it for a small palace. As usual with this style of architecture, the grounds were formal but immaculately kept. On the lawn in front of the chateau were two impressive fountains cascading water high into the air. What a location it was with the foothills of the Pyrenees rising steadily behind.

When we arrived, we were ushered in to see the two managers. They were both outwardly cheery but had worried frowns on their faces. They introduced themselves as Pascal and Louis. I began the conversation.

"We're both very pleased to meet you. My name is James and my friend here is Lord Bigsby. We are private detectives and we've been hired by Lady Helen Fairdown to enquire into the unexplained death of her husband, Lord Percy. We understand he owned this vineyard."

Both men gave unmistakable gasps. To my surprise, it was Bigsby, with his remarkable eyesight, who interrupted me.

"Please be honest with us as we're here to help and bring the killer of Lord Percy to justice. We do believe he was murdered. Am I correct in thinking that your *real* names are Jacques and Pierre as I can see slight patches of red hair underneath the black dye of one of you?"

"You're correct, Lord Bigsby. We are very worried for our lives and also for those of our wives. If anyone finds out who we are, we cannot bear to think of the consequences."

I continued with the conversation as Bigsby had by now looked out of the window and seen the rows of vines.

"Please don't worry too much, Jacques and Pierre, as we will do everything possible to ensure your safety. We thought you had been killed and buried at The Hut, which is situated in the mountains near Lourdes, but it turned out to be two men unknown to us.

"We've spoken to your wife, Jacques, and she told us you've been missing for over two years. Could you please tell us everything that's happened to you in the meantime and why you left Campan?"

"Certainly we will, Lord Bigsby and Field Marshal James," said Pierre, "as we're desperate to get back to the loves of our lives and our families. This is what happened. We'd just been banned from working or entering the Campan premises after five o'clock by Sir Clive Ponywood himself. This we agreed to, but on the third day, Jacques here had forgotten to give the cows their extra feed. He came and asked me if I'd go back to the Estate with him as he was a little afraid with the time being after five o'clock. There was no one about so we fed the cattle but as we got to the gate on our way home, we were apprehended and bundled into the back of a van."

"Do you mind if I interrupt a minute," I said. "Did you hear or see anything unusual while you were there?"

"We saw two men in white coats working at a bench in the new, large shed that had been recently erected. This we hadn't seen before."

"It all sounds very strange to me," I exclaimed.

Pierre continued, "We couldn't understand it either but can you imagine how petrified we were when they manhandled us into the back of a van? We were both certain our time was up! They then drove us to a small hidden parking place and bound our hands tightly and made us walk to an old shepherd's cottage in the hills. We were then thrown into the building and they barred the door. From the window, we saw Lord Percy painting in the distance.

"We were terrified! We could hear them digging and we knew they were digging what was supposed to be our grave. For a while after that everything was quiet. When we looked out of the window we saw them running hard after Lord Percy as though they wanted to apprehend him. We wondered if they were after the painting in case there was anything in it which might incriminate them.

"After an hour, they returned to let us out and marched us to the hole they had dug in the ground. They then announced with much laughter they were going to shoot us.

"They said they'd shoot Jacques first as he'd been so meek and had followed their instructions and said, because of this, they'd untie his hands before they shot him. This was their fatal error. Jacques may be thin and seem to have little strength, but he possesses a black belt in both karate and judo.

"After his arms were free, he was like lightening and two karate chops later, the man with the gun was unconscious, with the gun lying on the floor. Without hesitation, he picked it up and then shot the other man a number of times before shooting his first victim so as to make sure he was dead. I owe my life to good old Jacques here. Boy! He was as quick as a flash! Jacques had never handled a gun in his life before but, gosh, you'd never have known.

"We then put them in the hole they'd dug for us and after filling it in we made our way back to the road. We decided to take the van which we'd come in back and we left it about a couple of hundred yards from the entrance to Campan.

"We then received another fright as a car had stopped right by us but we need not have worried. It was the cheery face of Lord Percy asking what the so-and-so we were doing at that time of night. We warned him not to enter the Estate and advised him to come home with us where we'd tell him everything that had happened, but he thought it best for us to get in his car and tell him there."

I interrupted again as I saw Bigsby's mind was only half on the conversation while the other half was wondering if he'd be taken on a tour of the vineyard and allowed to sample some wine.

"Were you surprised to see Lord Percy at his Campan Estate at that time of year or was this one of his usual visits?"

"Yes, we were surprised. After we told him everything that had happened to us, he said he was staying a couple of nights at Toulouse regarding another venture in which he hoped we would join him as we'd been the only employees he could trust implicitly. He added that he couldn't go into any more detail at that moment.

"He then advised us to go to Toulouse with him where he would find us accommodations because he was sure if we stayed at our own home we'd soon be dead. This we did and he found us rooms in a small hotel in the centre of the town which was more than adequate for our needs. He told us not to return to our home near Lourdes but to let events take their course.

"We were worried about our wives, but he told us he was sure we'd meet up with them again one day and it was much wiser at the moment to concentrate on being safe. Lord Percy stayed in Toulouse for a couple of days and then told us he'd be returning within a month and, hopefully, he'd be able to offer us employment.

"He also advised us, as we were wanted men, to go under other Christian names, to alter out faces by growing beards, alter our hairstyles and, most importantly—for Jacques to dye his hair black."

"Were you both happy with this arrangement?"

"It was the only alternative we could see and to return back to our wives would have been very dangerous for them as well as us. Lord Percy returned to Toulouse after three weeks and offered us both work at Chamour as managers. We've been very happy in our work here although we both find more enjoyment in working with animals."

It was all very interesting hearing what they had to say and how Lord Percy had offered them protection. I continued the conversation.

"Did Lord Percy take you into his confidence at all after he'd offered you employment on his vineyard?"

"Yes, he did, Field Marshal James. He told us that we had always been honest and that our work at the Campan Estate had been exemplary. He said that others who he'd put faith in had all betrayed him."

"Did he give you any inclination why he'd sold the Campan Estate and bought Chamour?" I continued.

"He'd heard a rumour that the Campan Estate was being run partly for illegal profit but he didn't know in what way. He confided in us that nearly all the profit he'd accrued from the Estate had been withdrawn from the Campan Estate Bank Account in London over the past few months for unspecified reasons. Beside himself, Clive Ponywood was the only person who had the authority to withdraw money from this account.

"Because of the worry that the estate was causing him and something that he'd seen that had greatly worried him at Lourdes, he decided to sell the estate. He wanted no part in anything illegal. He told us that now that he had no more responsibilities in France, he was happy to forget the past apart from his desire to get even with Sir Clive.

"He was convinced that Sir Clive Ponywood, after all the trust he'd placed in him as overseer of the estate, had become a dangerous traitor. He said he was going back to London to engage a private detective to discover what activities Clive had been engaged in, but would be returning very shortly.

"This is the first we've heard about him since that day. Perhaps you could be those detectives for poor old Percy's sake. He gave us so much happiness by employing us in jobs we loved and we have great respect for him.

"As soon as Campan came on the market, a Spanish gentleman, named Baron de Buena, offered to purchase the Estate. Sir Clive was responsible for negotiations regarding the sale. Lord Percy eventually agreed with the Baron's demands to sell for half the market value. The financial loss didn't bother him as his over-riding desire was to get even with Sir Clive..

"We both pleaded with him not to take revenge but to concentrate on his vineyard because it's one of the finest in the area. As you can see, it's in the most scenic countryside location and I'm sure his family would have been delighted to live here.

"Jacques, who is the most peace-loving of men and would never bear a grudge, told Lord Percy that revenge would never give him a sense of closure and that it had the capacity to bring suffering to people he loved. But Lord Percy, although he respected Jacques' plea, would have none of it.

"Lord Percy told us he'd seen the Chateau about five years earlier. For him, it had a mystical, almost magical attraction. As well as the Baroque architecture, which he loved, the gardens held a special attraction.

"He said for the last few years, he'd deceived his family and badly let them down. He knew how his daughter Priscilla, such a country-loving girl, would enjoy Chamour and was confident that it was the perfect location for his family to settle.

"That's all we know."

"Do you know, Pierre, of any way we can find out what is going on at Campan?"

"We've been talking about this a lot and there's a possible way. Two of the horses, while we were still working at Campan, escaped from their enclosure. While rounding them up, we discovered a small, very overgrown cave at the bottom of a steep slope just outside the boundary fence. From here, we think it would be possible to get a good view of the estate buildings."

"That's a great idea and we'll look into it further when we come back in a few days-time."

I did not consider Jacques or Pierre were in any real danger at the moment, but seeing their worried faces, I told them that I'd have a word with General Couture, who was assisting us, about having a couple of guards who would discreetly protect them. I also told them that I thought it was necessary to take their wives to a place of safety and inform them about what was happening. They were more than happy with these arrangements.

"Would it be possible to have a quick tour of the vineyard before we go?" asked Bigsby. "I have a great interest in wine and viniculture. I'm a wine enthusiast. The more wine I drink, the more enthusiastic I get! Ha! We'll then go back to Champs, where we're staying, after we've taken your wives to a place of safety, to confer about what our next move should be. We'll be returning in a day or two," said Bigsby.

Bigsby was in his element having a private tour of the vineyard and even more so when they presented us with a case of twelve assorted bottles of wine. We thanked them for the wine and they wished us a safe journey and pleaded with us to come back as soon as possible and to make sure we gave their love to their wives.

Arriving back at Lourdes, our first duty was to go and visit the wives of Jacques and Pierre and to explain that their husbands were still alive and had protection and that they themselves needed to be taken to a place of safety for a few days. When we told Jacques' wife, Teresita, the news about their husbands, she was over the moon and ran to Pierre's wife, Simone, to tell her also.

What a scene for the next quarter of an hour as both ladies hugged each other, half laughing and half crying. We waited until they had both calmed down and then we explained the situation more fully.

We told them to get all the necessities they needed to last for a few days because they'd be returning with us to Champs where we would make sure they were safe. They were overwhelmed when they saw the beauty of Champs and realized it was to be their home for a short while.

When we arrived back, Couture was waiting for us and eager to know all the news. When we'd told him, he arranged for two female police officers to come and give protection to the ladies. It was after another brilliant meal, that we settled down to consider the possible actions we should now take.

The next day we set off back again for Chamour to explore the possibility of using the cave as a viewpoint with Jacques and Pierre. Bigsby said we would now have time to have a much more detailed tour of the vineyard. The viticulturist, Monsieur Vine, who'd attended to the vineyard for many years, agreed to show us around to explain the cultivation methods. Jacques and Pierre accompanied us.

Vine knew everything there was to know from both a practical and theoretical viewpoint and his enthusiasm sparked our interest in gaining greater knowledge of the subject. Before we started the tour, he gave us a brief summary as follows.

"Pruning of the vine is of the utmost importance as this is the only way to control the grape quality and the health of the vine. Just over ninety percent of the new growth is removed. One thousand four hundred hours of sunshine with around twenty-seven inches of rainfall is ideal with most of the rain falling in the winter or spring. You can see this vineyard is planted on a slight slope of the hillside as this means it receives more heat from the sun.

"The soil has to be of a good quality with good drainage being essential. One has always to be on the lookout for mildew and other diseases but with good management this can be controlled. Chardonnay, Pinot Noir and Shiraz are the main varieties of grape that we grow here. I will explain more fully as we go."

We then started our tour and one would have thought that Bigsby was on a viticulture course rather than on a murder hunt!

After returning to Chamour, we set off to investigate the location of the cave and if it was suitable for our needs.

Our access was from a minor road above the cave. From here, the limestone hillside sloped down six hundred metres to the perimeter fence of the Campan Estate. We descended half way down the slope where we could see the outline of the cave. The steep scramble meant we'd have to negotiate loose rock, moss, a mountain pine which had succumbed to the wind, hawthorn, elm and holly to name but a few..

It was certainly possible, with care, to reach the cave below. Here we'd be able to see directly into the shed when the doors were open.

"I'll leave this to you, James. Too tricky a scramble down for me!" said Bigsby.

Now that we knew the cave was accessible, we'd return to Champs to discuss what to do. We thanked Pierre and Jacques for showing us the way and told them we'd see them soon.

I suggested that Couture would be the best person to go down to the cave with me and watch. We eventually decided on this and to keep a look-out from ten o'clock in the morning to six o'clock at night. Our task then was to go into Toulouse on our way back to buy a powerful pair of binoculars. We finally decided on the most up-to-date Carl Zeiss Deltrintem 8x30 model. This would be ideal for our purpose.

On arrival back at Champs, we explained to Couture our plan and he was more than willing to come with me to the cave. The following day, Bigsby drove Couture and me to our starting point above the cave. He would return to collect us soon after six o'clock. It was indeed a tricky descent but, apart from a few scratches, we made it safely down.

A noise from nearby made our hearts miss a beat but we soon spotted the culprit. We'd startled a roe deer that had been quietly feeding. We did think for a second that it was a guard from Campan!

The entrance to the cave was virtually unidentifiable with a mass of flowers and fallen branches across the opening. Blackthorn and holly were growing here with an abundance of orchids, saxifrage and lilies. By removing two of the rotting branches near the ground, we were able to crawl in without much disturbance. What a splendid view we now had of the new shed at Campan.

The binoculars were first-class and it was easy to move away a little rotting vegetation from the cave entrance that allowed us to see through them clearly. For the first two hours, the shed doors remained closed and we saw no-one.

We spent the time watching the serins and black redstarts flying from bush to bush and the swifts flying in and out of the cave where they were nesting. A green lizard was sunning itself on a nearby rock while the coneys were busily nibbling on the grasses.

CHAPTER NINE

At two o'clock, the shed doors opened to reveal two men in white coats busy at a worktop inside. Looking intently through the binoculars, I instantly knew what they were doing.

I watched in disbelief. If anyone unauthorized saw this they would be immediately disposed of. Were Sir Clive Ponywood and his compatriot of the opinion that Jacques and Pierre had knowledge of this and ordered their killing? Did they think Lord Percy had seen this also? How long had they been producing heroin? What else could I deduce at the moment as it appeared so obvious? I passed the binoculars to Couture who was in complete agreement.

This is all we saw that day so at six o'clock we made our way up to the road where Bigsby was patiently waiting for us. I was unusually quiet on our return to Champs as I was still a little shocked from what I'd seen. Bigsby, bless his soul, must have realized this and, therefore, didn't try to enter into conversation.

We'd eaten very little so we decided to have our meal before we discussed matters. Afterwards we settled ourselves in a private lounge so that we couldn't be overheard. Bigsby was the first to speak.

"Well, James, give us the bad news. It must be something bad from your reaction."

"There were two men wearing white coats, which I took to be chemists, preparing some substance on a large worktop. I've seen illustrations very similar to this in the *London World Crime* magazine. I'm absolutely convinced, without a shadow of a doubt, that these two white-coated men were processing morphine base which they would have acquired from another country. Couture was sure of this also."

Bigsby interrupted. "What is morphine base, James, as I have never heard of it?"

"Opium is the dried latex which is acquired from the opium poppy. Just over ten per cent of this is made up of morphine which can be chemically processed to produce heroin. The opium poppy is grown in abundance in Turkey and Lebanon. If you had studied at Cambridge rather than spending all your lecture time at Oxford either on the shooting range or sports field you would have known that, my Lord."

"And you're sure they were processing it at Campan?"

"Very sure, Bigsby, because I saw the illustrations in that magazine I mentioned and also read about the processing method."

After a little discussion, we decided that I'd go back to the cave again the following day on my own and keep watch. Bigsby dropped me off again on the road above. The scramble down was easier this time as I now knew what to expect in terms of obstacles. As I neared the cave, a snake slithered through the grass. I was a little worried until I saw it was a harmless grass snake, maybe searching for a meal of lizard in the undergrowth.

Everything was quiet at the Estate when I arrived at ten o'clock. I saw and heard nothing until the shed door was again opened at two o'clock, probably to allow a little air to circulate. I could now see the two men busily working.

A little before four o'clock, there was action at last. A car drew up at the shed driven by a Spanish-looking man. In the passenger seat was another man.

The passenger descended from the car holding an orange pair of dungarees and took them inside the shed before returning a few moments later to the car. The car then drove away. Could the driver of the car have been the new owner, Baron de Buena?

All was then quiet and at six o'clock, I climbed back to the road where Bigsby was once again waiting. I told him what I'd seen. It all seemed very mysterious.

Back at Champs, Bigsby, of course, was more interested in the dinner and wine menus! Couture would be joining us at ten o'clock to discuss matters which gave us ample time for our meal.

"I was told yesterday, Bigsby, you have to open a bottle of wine to allow it to breath but if it doesn't look like it's breathing then to give it mouth to mouth. Ha! Ha!"

After Couture's arrival, we had another discussion about the production of heroin at Campan.

Bigsby asked how they were able to obtain the morphine base and why process it in such a remote place as the Agricultural Estate.

"Couture will have a much better idea but I'm of the opinion that they purchase the commodity from Turkey as this is one of the main places where the opium poppy is grown. The farmers there have a licence to grow opium poppies to supply legal drug companies but most will sell any excess to the black market. It'll then be shipped to one of the large ports nearby which I'm led to believe would be Marseilles. From there, Clive Ponywood would collect it and take it back with him.

With the customs men being fairly active at Marseilles, it's quite a risky undertaking. If caught, a person would spend a substantial number of years behind bars. The profits, if successful, would be staggering. Morphine base is normally processed in remote rural areas because of the strong distinctive smell that occurs while doing so. That's what I think at present, Bigsby. Couture is the expert on French matters so what are your thoughts on the matter, Couture?"

"I totally agree with you, James. Marseilles is the obvious port as ships dock there from Turkey and then they smuggle the heroin on boats bound for New York City in the United States of America. Here the substance is in high demand. As you say, it's a very risky business but with huge profits.

The question is, where do we go from here to apprehend them with this illegal substance in their possession? If we go into the Campan Estate with our men, I'm sure Ponywood will have contingency escape plans and then they'll be gone and to who knows where. I think we all need a good night's rest to refresh our minds for tomorrow."

After breakfast the next morning, we again settled in the private lounge to discuss matters. We'd been to see the wives of Jacques and Pierre earlier and they were in extremely good spirits knowing they would soon be reunited with their husbands after two long years.

"Have you any suggestions about our strategy?" I asked Couture.

"I'd imagine that Clive Ponywood would have acquired enough morphine paste to last for a few weeks, but I suggest he may be smuggling it to New York about every fortnight for financial reasons. If this is the case, it appears more likely that we'll have to apprehend him while he's delivering the heroin to the boat bound for America. What do you say, James?"

"I totally agree with you, Couture, as then the heroin can be traced back to its processing facility at Campan. It'll be easy to prove if it came from there as all heroin will have slightly different properties according to the individual processing method. Maybe a trip to Marseilles will be our next important step to allow us to enquire about the sailing time of boats to America and to study the general layout of the docks."

"Are there any vineyards near Marseille if we have the time to visit, Couture?" asked Bigsby. "Wine improves with age and I improve with wine. Ha! Ha!"

"It all depends when the next boat sails for America, if we have time or not, but Cassis is about thirty minutes away. Cassis is situated in a beautiful location and there's at least one small vineyard near the town which is the Clos Sainte Magdeleine where the cassis blanc and cassis rose wines are exceptional. The vineyards there are sheltered by the Cap Canaille which is the tallest coastal cliff in France at four hundred metres high."

Bigsby looked pleased so I did hope we could spare an hour or two to take a look around. It was arranged that we'd have a quiet day that day and make arrangements to go to Marseilles the following day and to start early and that Couture would accompany us.

Due to the distance, we would need to make an overnight stop, but we decided to get as far as possible before we did so. We stayed overnight approximately eighty miles from Marseilles so we were hoping to get there by mid-morning the next day.

We arrived the following day about eleven o'clock at Marseilles, which is France's biggest port. The two things that I always longed to see there were the Vieux Port which was guarded by the two massive forts of Fort Saint-Nicolas and Fort Saint-Jean and the Porte D'Aix which was a triumphal arch which paid homage to the French victories in the Spanish Expedition.

As we approached the harbour, Couture spoke. "A few hundred yards up here we'll leave the car and see if anyone can help us in relation to boats sailing to New York." After we got out of the car, we'd only walked five minutes before we heard Bigsby's urgent whisper.

"Shh!! Quick, behind here! Don't look back! The person speaking to that official over there on the quayside is the spitting image of those I've seen of Clive Ponywood. He may have heard about us and be on the lookout so we'd better be ultra-cautious. It could turn out to be a massive stroke of luck for us, though, if it is him."

"Let me take a quick look," said Couture. "It's the harbour-master, Francois Drake, he's speaking to. I know him reasonably well so we can go and speak to him after Clive—if it is Clive—is well out of the way."

We watched them both from a position where we couldn't be seen. Clive, as we assumed he was, handed the harbour-master a small package before he departed in the other direction and out of sight.

We all looked at each other in wonder. It was Couture who was the first to speak.

"It looks like he's bribed poor old Francois. Let's go and have a word with him. If we find out he has, then we'll have his co-operation. He'll have to tell us everything he can or I'll threaten him with arrest for taking bribes. I'll have you both as witnesses. Come on and I'll confront him."

Couture greeted Francois. "Well, if it isn't my old friend Francois! You're looking well these days and I see you have been promoted to harbour-master. Congratulations on that, my old friend."

"I'm so proud to be the harbour-master of France's biggest commercial port. I love my work, especially seeing the port expanding year by year. How are you, General Couture, and what brings you to Marseilles?"

"I'm here with my friends Lord Bigsby and Field-Marshal James, who are now private detectives, and are investigating a murder which was committed in England."

"If there's anything I can help you with, I will certainly do so."

"Thank you, as there is certainly information about shipping times which my friends would like from you and anything else which may be relevant to their enquiries. You must be quite wealthy now that you are the harbour-master," said Couture while tapping the pocket of Francois where the package was concealed.

His manner changed instantly. He gave the impression of a troubled man as he began to tremble.

"Please, General Couture, come into my office and I'll explain everything. I've been under so much strain during the past four months that I feel as though I'm having a nervous breakdown. My wife even keeps asking me if I am unwell."

Couture was taken aback, but responded with compassion. "Francois, I've known you and your wife for many years. I've always found you both to be honest and upright people and, indeed, the salt of the earth. I'm sure if you have done wrong you've been under intense pressure to do so. If this is the case, and you co-operate fully with me and my friends, we will help you in every way possible."

Francois burst into tears as he replied, "Thank you so much, General Couture. My work here gives me so much pleasure and great fulfillment as I see the port developing its facilities."

"Don't worry, as your work here as harbour-master will be totally safe if you've done no wrong. Come, please tell us everything."

"Well, General Couture, it all began about four months ago when someone, who introduced himself as Sir Clive Ponywood, accused me of having an affair with the wife of the captain of a small fishing boat which is moored here. He said he'd seen me on several occasions having sex with her in a small abandoned shed in a disused area of the harbour and that he'd seen me attempt to push her husband into the sea on one occasion. It came as a complete shock to me.

"As you know, General Couture, I'd never betray my wife and family as they are precious to me. If I didn't obey his commands faithfully, he said he would tell my wife everything and also would report me to the police. I was devastated and totally confused with these pre-fabricated lies intending to blackmail me into doing something illegal.

"Even though there was no semblance of truth in anything he said, it meant I would lose my job here, which I love so much, nor would I be able to support my family in the way that I do now. In the end, I had no option but to acquiesce to his demands. What a relief you have come."

I took over the conversation. "Relax, Francois, as all we want is to bring Ponywood to justice and then your life can carry on as happily as before. Firstly, could you please explain why Ponywood was here today and what he was planning."

"Yes, Field Marshal James. He came to make sure of the times of the arrival and departure of a boat to New York. This boat, The New Horizon, is due to depart in five days at 11.00 a.m. on Saturday morning. Sir Clive arrives here dressed in large orange dungarees, with heroin concealed in pockets which have been sewn inside them, and goes into my office.

At a pre-arranged time, about three hours before the boat sails, the purser of The New Horizon also comes into my office wearing identical dungarees and then these are exchanged between the two. It does seem a simple and ingenious way of smuggling goods. The purser confided in me that he was also bribed to do this in a similar way and that he too was very afraid for his life as these drug gangs are ruthless people. Could you please help him also? The bribe that Sir Clive gave me was for the use of my office where they could change their dungarees."

I told Francois that we would do everything in our power to help the purser. I then asked if he knew about Ponywood's travel arrangements from the Campan Estate to Marseilles and also if he travelled alone.

"He did mention to me that he always drove overnight. He also travelled alone."

I thanked him for all the information he'd given us and assured him that Clive Ponywood would no longer be interfering in his life. Couture told Francois that he'd have some of his men near his office on Saturday and that he'd contact the New York police to ensure the safety of the purser and his family. Francois looked a very relieved man as he wished us *au revoir*.

"Thank you. Merci, messieurs, vous êtes si bon pour moi. Merci beaucoup, mes amis."

As we drove away, I considered the dangers of heroin. Its effect caused severe mood swings as well as inducing irresponsible and threatening behaviour. Happy marriages and family life could easily be destroyed. Soon addiction would be reached with the high cost of the heroin leading to crime for financial gain.

More serious crime would ensue. Those who take heroin are often associated with violence and the use of guns, leading to traumatic effects on society. Happy peace loving people with their lives ruined.

What kind of person could produce heroin and sell it for financial gain knowing the misery and the terrible hurt it would cause? Surely, only people with an unquenchingly sinful lust for power and wealth. Oh! If only man could live in peace.

CHAPTER TEN

Bigsby insisted that we should have a couple of hours relaxation and visit the vineyard at Cassis as we'd have a very hectic three day schedule ahead of us. Bigsby would always insist if we were going to a vineyard! I'd already seen the Vieux Port and the Port D'Aix so now it was the wine expert's turn to enjoy himself.

He was a little disappointed to begin with as he was a red wine aficionado, but after tasting the very high quality Cassis Blanc and Cassis Rosé, he vowed to ask the sommelier at The Club to order a few cases. Unfortunately, we didn't have time to tour the vineyards as we had lots of planning to do when we arrived back at Champs.

We made a mental note of the roads and the towns and villages we'd passed through on our way back, and decided to have an overnight stop at Carcassonne as it was getting late. The old walled city, perched high on the hill, with its assortment of drawbridges, towers and cobbled streets, looked magical. It had certainly been an eventful day.

We arrived back at Champs about mid-day which gave us a good two days to devise a strategy where we could detain Clive Ponywood in possession of the heroin destined for New York.

We opened out a map of the road between Lourdes and Marseilles and hoped that one of us would come up with some brilliant idea. Bigsby asked me what my thoughts were on the subject. I was sure his thoughts were mostly on the vineyard at Cassis and why he'd always deemed white wines inferior to red wines.

"I suppose we have three options, my Lord," I said, "and then we'll have to consider which one will be the most effective by examining their advantages and disadvantages.

"We can apprehend Ponywood at Campan Estate prior to leaving for Marseilles, while he's traveling there, or after his arrival at the port. My choice would be to somehow stop him while enroute so he'd have to abandon his car. What do you think, Bigsby?"

"I think it's been foolish of me to think of white wines in the way I have. Oh, I mean, yes, I agree with you, James. If we try to accost him at Campan, he'll have plenty of time to hide the heroin and the morphine base. I'm sure he's made contingency plans for this. There are three locked gates before we could get to the processing shed, so that way seems impossible. I'm sure Couture will agree."

"Yes, I'm sure he will," said Bigsby, "so that now leaves us with two options. Like you, I'm of the opinion that apprehending him at the port may cause further problems as it will be a very bustling place prior to the boat sailing for New York. Ponywood would probably claim that he was innocent and that he'd been exploited by a member of a drug's gang. Well, James, what next?"

"The best option I can think of is for us, somehow, to stop the car on the road a few miles from Marseilles and prevent it making further progress. I'm sure that by this time Ponywood will have donned his dungarees in case of any unforeseen problems at the port preventing him from doing so. Dressed in his dungarees, with the heroin hidden inside, we'll catch him red-handed and he'll have no means of escape.

"Looking further at the map, I'd suggest that somewhere in the region of the city of Arles would be a good place. I suggest we drive there to see if we can work out a plan on how to do this. In relation to vineyards, my dear Bigsby, Arles is where Vincent Van Goch painted one of his major works, 'The Red Vineyards Near Arles', which was his only painting to be sold during his lifetime."

"What was the point of painting if he didn't make money from it, James?"

"A very sad story indeed from what I learned from my studies at Cambridge. A genius who created about 2,100 artworks but was still considered a madman. He suffered from mental illness and committed suicide at the age of thirty-seven. Well, Bigsby, what do you think about my plan?"

"It's the only workable solution that I can see and I'm sure Couture will agree. We'll start off early tomorrow and devise our strategy while we are there."

In truth, Couture did agree with our plan. We set off for Arles early the next day as time was now of the essence. We'd given ourselves two options. The vehicle that Clive Ponywood was traveling in had either to be stopped on the road that followed the coast between Beziers and Montpellier, or the inland road between Montpellier and Arles.

One of the prominent buildings we saw at Arles was the two-tiered Roman Amphitheatre built in 90 A.D. with its one hundred and twenty arches which appears to have been inspired by the Colosseum in Rome. It was constructed to provide entertainment of the likes of chariot racing and hand-to-hand bloody battles. Now it draws large crowds for bullfighting during the Feria d'Arles as well as plays and concerts in the summer. I'd never imagined that this area of France was so rich in historic sites, from Roman ruins to medieval fortresses.

We stopped for lunch at the bull-fighting town of Beziers for an hour to relax. After this, we traversed the road between Beziers and Arles a number of times to allow us to make a final decision. Finally, after spending four hours examining the road, we stopped at a Chateau at Montpellier for the night, much to the delight of Bigsby.

After we'd all given our individual opinions, we found we were totally in agreement. Montpellier, built on rising ground on the River Lez, is a university city and boasts the oldest, still-active medical school in Europe.

We had now made up our minds. After having made a final examination of our chosen spot where we hoped to immobilize the vehicle of Clive Ponywood, we returned back to Champs.

Once back, we had no time to waste as we settled down in the private lounge. Couture then asked me what kind of action did I think was the best to apprehend Ponywood with his stash of heroin.

"My initial way of thinking would be for myself and Bigsby to wait in the car where we have a good view of the main road, just off a side-road that goes down to the tiny fishing village of Meze, until Ponywood passes in his vehicle. We would immediately follow him.

"At a quiet spot a few miles further on, near the small commune of Poussan, Bigsby would blow one of the back tires in Ponywood's vehicle with a shot from his Walther. What happens after this, I don't know, but at least we'll have the upper hand. What usually happens in France in a scenario such as this, Couture?"

"In the normal course of events, the suspected criminals would give themselves up as they wouldn't want a charge of murder or causing actual bodily harm added to their drug dealing crime. They'd know if they co-operated with the police, that the sentence given by the judge would not be too great. I suspect Ponywood will do the same."

I asked Bigsby his view on the subject.

"This sounds the best possible way to go about it and I only hope we don't get into a shooting match. Will you be right behind us with your men, Couture?"

"Yes, Bigsby; I'll bring two trusted men with me and we'll be immediately behind you in case of trouble. Tomorrow is Friday, so I suggest that we travel to Beziers tomorrow and spend the night there.

"At three o'clock in the morning, you and James will leave and we'll follow shortly after. It'll give you ample time then to be waiting down the side-road to Meze as early as four o'clock. I'd expect them to pass by about five o'clock, but who knows? You and James will take a marked police car so Ponywood will have no doubt who's following him."

With a little fear and trepidation, we left Champs for Beziers the next morning. As Bigsby's luck would have it, there was a large signpost pointing the way to a vineyard only one mile from the town! We had a meal here and Bigsby, to my great surprise, bought a bottle of Sauvignon and a bottle of Chardonnay. He really was becoming a white wine connoisseur! We refrained from any alcohol while there so as to stay alert for what lay ahead.

After we'd eaten, we looked for a small hotel where we could get some rest until the early hours of the morning when the action would begin in earnest. At three o'clock in the morning, Bigsby and I rose to get ready for what we hoped would be a reasonably peaceful confrontation with Clive Ponywood. Bigsby made sure his Walther was ready and loaded as he was taking no chances. We'd been given authority, through General Couture, to shoot in the case of self-defence.

It was only a short drive to the turn off to Meze and we parked the car about a hundred yards down this road where we had a clear view of all the cars passing by on the road to Marseilles. All we could do now was to wait for Ponywood's vehicle. Although we were expecting no trouble, our hearts were starting to beat faster and we were getting more and more apprehensive by the minute.

We could hear the gulls circling over the fishing port of Meze, the oyster capital of the area. What would I have given to go down to the harbour and buy half a dozen oysters! To shuck them and eat them raw is a culinary delight for me. A real taste of the sea!

"I think we should start the engine now, James, as we don't want to be caught unaware. It's now five o'clock and we estimated they'd be driving by before six. When you have the opportunity to get very close behind them, I'll flash the 'Police Stop' sign. If they continue without slowing, I'll blow out one of the back tires with my Walther."

Fifteen minutes later, Clive Ponywood went by and we immediately followed. There was, fortunately, very little traffic on the road. After a few minutes, I'd picked up enough speed to get very close behind him and for him to be sure it was a police car ordering him to stop. His reaction, though, was to increase speed and there was no sign of him heeding our warning.

This was unexpected and I could now sense danger not far away. Eventually, Bigsby had no option but to blow out a tire to force him to stop. He was as accurate as ever even though both cars were moving at speed. Ponywood's car swerved towards the grass verge but he expertly kept it under control. Caution was the watchword now.

"When I stop the car, Bigsby, run for the shelter of those two rocks on the seaward side and make no delay. I have a strange feeling he may open fire."

As soon as we'd reached the safety of the rocks, we could see Ponywood opening fire indiscriminately, but nowhere near where we were. He then ran, with his gun drawn, towards the commune of Loupian.

"Fire a warning shot," I said to Bigsby. The shot echoed with a menacing sound around the countryside and immediately we saw Ponywood keep running until he reached the trees.

"We'll follow him, but make a detour to the right, James. That way he won't be able to shoot directly at us. You make for that broken-down stone wall by the big oak trees and you'll be safe for the moment. I'll make a dash for the wall at the edge of the field where I'll have a better view. Stay put unless I tell you otherwise."

You have to hand it to Bigsby. He may not be the most academically gifted person, but he is certainly the first to volunteer when there's danger. He's confident of his shooting ability, especially with his trusty Walther and those eagle eyes of his.

He dived down behind the wall at the same moment as a shot rang out with another closely following. Ponywood must have seen Bigsby as he dove for cover, but I couldn't tell if he was only firing as a warning or whether he was unaccustomed to using guns. His next shot was also off target, but I saw Bigsby's gun drop from his hand as he gave an anguished scream. The shot appeared to have ricocheted off a stone and then onto Bigsby's wrist and given him a very painful blow. *What if his wrist had been broken and he was unable to shoot?* I wondered. We would both be dead men soon. I was scared.

With hardly a pause, though, Bigsby picked up the gun in his left hand and moved quickly along the wall where he had a better view of his opponent. Ponywood lost sight of him for a moment. It was then that Bigsby, now left-handed, fired. I hardly dared look but the shot went straight at Ponywood's shoulder and he dropped the gun instantly. He must have been in agony as he came running towards us for help.

"I thought we were dead when your wrist was injured. Shooting with your left hand! What skill, my Lord! Is your wrist badly injured?"

"It appears to be badly swollen and is rather painful but fine otherwise. It means I'll have to hold my wine glass in my left hand for a couple of weeks!"

"How were you able to be so accurate with your other hand?"

"Don't forget, James, I didn't waste my time at Oxford learning all this academic stuff. I spent my lecture hours on the shooting range where I became rather proficient with both hands. I bet you're thankful for that now, James, my friend."

I certainly was! On the way back to our car, we saw Ponywood running towards us trembling and in tears. He looked like a broken man so, giving him the benefit of the doubt, we treated him with a little compassion and took him back with us to the car. He pleaded his innocence and maintained he'd been blackmailed into it. This was plausible but we'd find out soon enough.

"What happened to Couture and those two strong armed men of his? Terrified of a bit of danger, I bet. They said they'd be right behind us and protect us. Some protection!" scoffed Bigsby.

"Ah! Here they are, driving towards us now, Bigsby. Some use to us coming over half an hour too late! Bet they have some lame excuse. Maybe drunk too much of that wine you bought yesterday!"

Couture alighted the car full of apologies. "What a relief to find you both safe. Our car wouldn't start when we got in it at the hotel. We summoned a mechanic immediately and only a few minutes ago has it been repaired. Who is this miserable looking person sitting in your car and where is Ponywood? Has he got away?"

I responded, rather sarcastically, "Thanks for your help, Couture, which we really appreciated. It was only Bigsby and his amazing shooting skills that saved us. The person here is Ponywood and he was shot in the shoulder by Bigsby in self-defence and is writhing in agony sitting in the car. As you can observe, Bigsby's wrist is very swollen so we need to get off to the hospital at Montpellier immediately for it to be x-rayed."

"You both acted bravely and with great courage. We'll now see to matters here while you go to Montpellier and then we'll meet you back at Champs to discuss the course of events. Tell

Ponywood to get in our car and you two continue on your way with the police car."

We drove on to the hospital at Montpellier to have Bigsby's wrist examined and treated. As we were turning into the entrance, something clicked in my brain. As Bigsby was being treated by Dr. Andre Mendit, I jokingly told him that I'd have a tour of one of the local vineyards. He was on the point of exploding! Instead, I went to see the Hospital Registrar to see if my intuition which had just occurred to me, was correct.

Bigsby's wrist had not been broken but badly bruised. He was advised to rest it for a few days. On leaving the hospital, we thought it wise to go on to Marseilles for a quick word with Francois to assure him that all was now well. He was very grateful.

"Thank you so much and now I can get back to enjoying my life with my family which is more precious to me than gold. How can people like Ponywood illegally smuggle drugs into another country to make vast amounts of money without thinking about the consequences it has on the naive people who take them? It's awful to think how many loving families will be split up because of the indiscriminate use of these drugs.

"Family life should be the bedrock of society and I know how much you both care about yours. Please come and visit us and meet my wife whenever you are in the area again. How fortunate I have been to have met you both."

We left a happy Francois standing overlooking the port that he loved and had helped so much in its expansion. It was now time to make haste back to Champs to meet up with Couture.

CHAPTER ELEVEN

It was late when we arrived back, and a message was waiting for us to say that General Couture would meet us the following morning. Although dinner had already been served, the chef at Champs willingly served up his usual gourmet fare for us. After a few drinks, we were beginning to relax and recover from our ordeal. We were too exhausted to think, so we retired to bed.

Over a late breakfast the following morning, we discussed the happenings of the previous day and where it was likely to lead us.

"I'm sure, Bigsby, that Couture will want us to go with him to examine the Campan Estate to see what we can unearth and search for evidence of the heroin being produced from the morphine base. I also wonder what else we'll find. Ah! Here he is now."

"Bonjour, mes amis! I will explain all that happened after we left Sir Clive yesterday. He is now being kept in police custody until the drug smuggling investigations are complete. Unless his innocence is proved, he will then be sent for trial."

As we expected, Couture asked us to go with him on his visit to Campan. When we arrived, the guard at the gate was reluctant to let us through until we showed him our identification and the court order to allow us to search the premises. We were allowed to pass through the other two gates without any problem. We parked the car by the door of the big shed.

Two men in white coats, presumably chemists, were working near the entrance. They told us, quite openly, that they'd been employed to process the morphine base into heroin. They had accepted the job because they had been unemployed and because the pay was good.

We could see that alterations to the shed were taking place with a large hidden workshop being constructed below the ground floor. Expansion plans were certainly in progress. In a smaller room, a dozen paintings were discovered which reminded me of some of the old masters. We were all puzzled by this. One of the paintings caught my eye and I asked Couture if I could take it back to Champs and examine it more closely, which he allowed me to do.

We found nothing else to suggest that other illegal activities had taken place here, so we headed back to what we now referred to as home.

Couture had left to authorize and conduct full enquiries into how the morphine base had been smuggled in, how it had been processed, and where it was destined for. An enquiry, I assume, that would take several weeks.

"Well, James, seeing we've excelled in finding the killer of Lord Percy, you don't look like you're sharing the same elation and sense of satisfaction that I am. Now we've nothing more to do here. I suggest we make an early start for home tomorrow to pass the good news on to Lady Helen. Then we can spend a few full days with our families."

After I'd responded with a barely audible grunt of acknowledgement, Bigsby continued speaking.

"What's the matter, James, my friend? Are you unwell or still in a state of shock?"

"Excelled? What do you mean? We don't have any proof at all that Clive was smuggling drugs or was involved in Sir Percy's murder. Innocent until proven guilty, my Lord

"It's my academically inquisitive mind and I still need proof. We don't have any firm evidence, that a court of law would accept, for the reason that Clive Ponywood murdered Sir Percy. There's a lot of circumstantial evidence, but that would not be accepted as proof. There's something nagging at the back of my mind. After dinner, I'm going to spend a few hours on my own going over everything we've uncovered in our investigation to date. I'll try to sort out and rationalize everything in my own mind. I'd like to spend tomorrow here so as to enable me to visit Lourdes and the immediate area. Hopefully, this will bring back to mind anything I may have regarded as of no consequence in relation to our murder hunt."

The following morning, Bigsby was eager to know what my opinions were.

"Here's a piece of paper on which I have written down a number of things we don't know and I think it necessary we should do our utmost to find out."

Bigsby took the paper which read as follows:

1. Do we know who Clive Ponywood really is?
2. Did he actually start to breed horses?
3. Was he the head of the smuggling operation?
4. Would the head act as a courier?
5. Do we know who Sir Martin really is?
6. Why were we sure initially he was a liar?

7. Who gave orders for Jacques' and Pierre's killing?

8. Who killed the two friends of Carolee?

9. Why were works of art stored in the big shed?

"See how little we really know, Bigsby. It's only our assumption that Clive killed Lord Percy. I'd still like a day around Lourdes today to see if we have overlooked anything there. We need to carry on with the investigation."

"I understand what you mean, James. The head of a drug operation would be the mastermind and not be involved in collecting or delivering the drugs from the port. So Clive may be just an unwilling assistant.

"When he was shooting at us after we blew out his car tire, I'm sure he had no intention of harming us. I could see by the way he was holding the gun that he was shooting deliberately wide and that's why I only incapacitated his shooting arm. The shot that injured my wrist was a ricochet from a rock and a complete fluke."

"I consider a trip to Barcelona and the offices of Taraya Estate Properties our first place of call. A meeting with Clive is also very important. He may have a perfectly good explanation for his actions.

"The reason that I'd like to meet with Neric Taraya again is that we may be able to discover more about Sir Martin. Their auction company in London would have done intensive research into his past before employing him. Maybe he also went under the name of Baron de Buena. Anyway, we'll go tomorrow to Barcelona. Would you, my Lord, speak to Couture so that he can arrange for us to interview Clive on our return?"

I spent the rest of that day visiting places around Lourdes and engaging as many people as I could in conversation. I was told where the late boyfriend of Carolee lived and as the door was open and no-one inside, I had a thorough look around. The house was very sparsely furnished.

Two things that did take my eye were an eighteenth century secretary writing desk in the regency style and a French Breton dining table with four chairs. These were in superb condition apart from scratches down one side of the writing desk. I would have loved to own them. I then returned to Champs to find Bigsby sampling white wine.

We were looking forward to our drive through the Pyrenees to Barcelona. It was a spectacularly bright and sunny day. We could clearly see Aneto, which holds the largest glacier in the Pyrenees on its northern side, and the nearby peaks of Maladeta and Pico del Medio amongst others. A bronze statue of Christopher Columbus atop a large monument greeted us as we entered Barcelona.

We stopped the car by the offices of Taraya Estate Properties and were warmly greeted by our young friend, Neric.

"Nice to see you again, and what brings you to Barcelona this time? Come into my office and tell me. I think it must be the wine, Bigsby!"

Bigsby nodded to me to explain our visit.

"You know, Neric, we're investigating the death of Lord Percy. Lady Helen, his wife, got married again to a person named Sir Martin Nash, who I gather has been in the employ of Peregrino Auction Services—your sister company—for a number of months. We've been reappraising everything we've gathered so far in our investigation and we now realize we know very little about Sir Martin. I understand your company does very thorough checks on all their employees and we were hoping you'd be free to tell us all you know about him."

"As this is a murder investigation, most certainly I will. We do hold a file here on all the people who are employed in London. Let me see now. Here it is—the file of Sir Martin. Oh dear!"

"What's the matter Neric?" I said. He was standing motionless, staring at the files with a stunned expression.

"I'm sorry to tell you that, when he returns to work after his enforced absence in relation to your investigation, he will be dismissed immediately without further remuneration."

Bigsby sat bolt upright and I just sat there gaping and momentarily speechless.

"What did you find out, Neric, that forces him to be dismissed? We were of the opinion that he was in the process of taking the company to new heights."

"Yes, the company has prospered because of Sir Martin but, unfortunately, we soon became aware of illegal dealings. We found that four of the paintings he included for auction were fakes. Although of superb quality there was no doubt in the mind of the expert that examined them that they were not by the signed artist."

I was sure I'd seen some paintings which I vaguely recognized at the big shed on the Campan Estate.

"Was one of the fake paintings purporting to be by Charles-Francois Daubigny by any chance?" I asked.

"Yes it was. Why do you ask, James?"

"Would you mind if I keep this information to myself as it may be crucial to our enquiries?"

"Not at all. What more did we find out about Sir Martin? We, at the company, have always looked into the background of any new employee but in this case we had to hire a special investigator as we came across many false leads in our attempt to trace his past. He was born into a middle class family in the Midlands and won a scholarship to Oxford where he gained a first-class honours degree in the history of art which eventually led to him achieving a doctorate.

"His main interest at Oxford was in amateur dramatics, with a special interest in the Shakespearean plays. He was President of the Amateur Dramatic Club for four years.

"He attempted to start a number of businesses, one of which was an auction house, but none succeeded. He had a brilliant mind and was an organizer with great innovative ideas. His businesses all failed because his practical sense was nearly zero. The last our investigator could find out about Sir Martin was that he was married to Lady Helen. As you know, he then began work for the Peregrino Auction Services in London. That is all that's recorded on the file and I hope it's been some help to you."

"Very much so, Neric. It has certainly changed the course of our enquiry when we thought it was all cut and dried and we had apprehended the murderer. By the way, was Claude Monet another of the artists whom someone had tried to fake?"

"Yes. It sounds like you're on the track of the faker so please keep us posted."

We assured him we would and said our farewells and left, very much deep in thought.

"Well, James, it appears it has been a very wise move coming to see Neric. Could Sir Martin be the bad guy?"

"After our first meeting with him when we regarded him with much suspicion, it's very possible that he could have duped us also. As President of the Oxford University Amateur Dramatic Society, his acting skills must have been highly regarded. I do hope for Lady Helen's sake, he is of genuine reputation."

"What now, James?"

"We will stay in Barcelona for the night as it's now getting late and tomorrow we'll have to go back to Champs to think. So much has changed in the last couple of hours. Clive is surely a blackmailer but he may not be a murderer. Who knows anymore?"

We spoke very little that night and also on the return trip to Champs. I was the first to bring up the subject after dinner that evening.

"Carolee is a genius when it comes to art. I recall she was at her easel when we first met her and the colour and vivacity in her painting was awe-inspiring in quality. Although it was not an exact copy of a Monet, it would have been very difficult to distinguish it from one as the quality and detail was comparable, if not more so, to that of the impressionist painter himself. Is it possible that Carolee faked the paintings that Sir Martin sold at auction?"

CHAPTER TWELVE

There was a letter waiting for us the following morning to say that Couture had obtained permission for us to visit Clive at any time. "I'm sure a trip to the police cells at Montpellier will be our task for tomorrow, Bigsby."

"Hopefully we can also make time to visit the vineyard at Montpellier where we had our meal and I purchased the white wines from. Surely, James, we deserve a couple of hours rest to have a tour and sample more wines. I'm now beginning to get obsessed with white wines."

We were really getting to appreciate the countryside of this area of the south of France and the grandeur of the Pyrenees. What a difference this was to the bustling streets of London. We thoroughly enjoyed our journey to Montpellier.

To put Bigsby in a happy frame of mind for our encounter with Sir Clive, I stopped at the vineyard where he'd purchased his white wines a few days previously. We both enjoyed our tour around with the viticulturist and the knowledgeable way he explained the husbandry of the vines. We were beginning to get as interested in the cultivation of the grapevine, and the characteristic of each variety of grape as we were in drinking the finished product.

Now it was down to business and our interview with Sir Clive. Maybe we would have a scientific discourse on the breeding of racehorses!

We stopped the car at the entrance to the police station and were directed to the cells where Sir Clive was being kept. As we entered his cell, we were struck with horror at the scene before us.

I had to start the conversation as I saw that Bigsby was still gazing open-mouthed and speechless.

"Don't be afraid, Sir Clive, if you're innocent of any wrong-doing. We're very close now to apprehending the murderer of Lord Percy."

Sir Clive was sprawled on the floor, howling like a two-year old deprived of his toys, and looked very close to death. According to the police officer who we'd spoken to on arrival, he hadn't eaten for three days and had drunk very little. They were planning to transfer him to the hospital later in the day.

Bigsby, who possessed a very compassionate heart, had already hurried out for a word with the police clerk to enquire if a meal could be brought as quickly as possible for Sir Clive. We then sat in silence until the food arrived.

With Sir Clive knowing we were there to help, he soon devoured the food that had been brought for him. Bigsby went out to the car and returned with a bottle of his precious white wine. What had come over him! A couple of mugs were brought for us and the wine was shared around. It certainly did the trick as Sir Clive stopped weeping and was starting to look more like a human being and happy to speak with us.

Had he been acting to try and persuade us of his innocence? Who knew anymore? If so, he had surpassed the acting skills of the rising duo of Laurel and Hardy. But we weren't going to take any chances.

Sir Clive began to speak in heart breaking, anguished tones.

"I'm so sorry. I panicked when you blew the tire out with your shot. I was sure it was Baron de Buena going to kill me and that he'd hijacked a police car so I'd give myself up easily. I made sure my shots were well wide as they were only meant as warning shots. I was terrified beyond belief. I would kill no one."

"I know that, Clive, and that' why I only shot to disarm you and not to kill but please tell us of your worries. I'm sure they're connected to the murder of Lord Percy," said Bigsby.

"I'm so happy you've come, Lord Bigsby and Field Marshal James. I became great friends with Lord Percy over twelve years ago while he was on holiday in Sussex. He had no enthusiasm for horses before he met me but my love for racing and the welfare of the racehorses certainly won him over. We spent many happy days together at Goodwood Racecourse while he was there on holiday.

"A few months later, he approached me to say that there was an agricultural and horse breeding estate for sale in the Pyrenees about which he had made enquiries and would I be prepared to join him in the venture."

"What was your reaction to this, Clive?" I asked.

"I was ecstatic beyond belief. It was a dream come true to breed thoroughbred horses and I accepted his offer immediately. I possess a personality disorder which only allows me to cope when I'm with animals or very close friends and relations. Both my parents had recently passed away and I was so happy to gain the friendship of Lord Percy. I had no other friends. When I'm with people I don't know or trust, I panic and often act irrationally. After my parents died, I had no-one I could confide in and since the death of Lord Percy I again have no friends."

"I'm so sorry to hear this. Did you find your work on the Campan Estate rewarding?" I interrupted.

"They were the best years of my life. Lord Percy was so supportive and with my knowledge of the best bloodlines, I bred horses which won some of the major races. Campan was slowly becoming a place where the serious owners came to buy thoroughbreds and financially we were doing very well. Then everything went wrong and my happy and fulfilling life crumbled underneath me. I was distraught and with no friends to turn to, I panicked and quickly became a nervous wreck."

"How long ago was this, Clive, and what happened?" I asked.

"For nine years, I built up the breeding side of Campan while also overseeing the farming side. The farming side entailed very little work as the two managers, Jacques and Pierre, were knowledgeable, hardworking and very conscientious. They both left suddenly, but I don't know for what reason. Big changes then took place, which are not yet complete. Baron de Buena informed me that the breeding side of Campan was being discontinued and all the horses were being sold."

At this point, Clive broke down in tears so I waited a few minutes for him to compose himself before I spoke to him again.

"What was your reaction to this and what was your role at Campan after the horses were sold?"

"I told Baron de Buena that as I owned all the horses, it would be illegal for him to sell them. He laughed at me and said from now on I had to do what I was told. I was often made to go to Marseilles to collect a package from a boat from Turkey. Other times, I had to go to Marseilles wearing oilskins and to make arrangements to exchange my oilskins for that of a sailor on a boat which was sailing to New York. I had to make sure everything was done secretly so I had to bribe the Harbour-master to help me.

"He would not be bribed so I had to threaten him before he would help. I felt so sorry for him and I do hope I can get the opportunity to apologize to him some time and repay him for what I did. I was a broken man. I was inhumane. I was just a despicable zombie. I'm sure what I was carrying were drugs but no one told me and I didn't ask."

Clive told us that his journeys to Marseille had been going on for nearly eighteen months and he was so thankful to see us and he pleaded with us to help him.

"Please help me, Lord Bigsby and Field Marshal James. I do apologize deeply for all the trouble and hurt I've caused, but I was so alone and terrified beyond belief."

Bigsby responded to his plea. "Clive, we're sure you've been honest in what you've told us and we thank you for this as it has helped our investigation greatly. James is sure that he'll have the necessary evidence to apprehend the murderer of Lord Percy within a few days.

"We don't have the power to release you from here until then, but please promise me that you'll try to regain your strength by taking proper meals during this time. If you're innocent, as we suspect, what help would you like us to give you?"

"All I require, Lord Bigsby, is to be able to work with horses again and to have a friend I can trust implicitly to whom I can turn for help when I need it. I have no interest whatsoever in money or wealth.

"Would you also be willing to assist me in locating the whereabouts of my beloved horses? Three of them have already won big races and I had high hopes of most of the others. The younger horses were progressing superbly.

"I'm sure there was a criminal mastermind directing the illegal operations at Campan and it's my view that the abduction of high class racehorses was a big part of his crime portfolio. Baron de Buena did appear to have absolute power at Campan but I don't know if he was the mastermind. I saw very little of him.

"If you do decide to help, please be aware that it will be a very dangerous task and your lives could be at stake. I'm more than willing to help as I'm prepared to lay down my life rather than see the horses suffer.

"All the registration documents and other papers relating to the horses are kept in my office at Campan. I also keep copies in a safe hidden under the bottom of the wardrobe in my bedroom at home."

"We will seriously consider helping you, Clive," I said. "I'll go over everything relating to our investigation so far with Bigsby tonight and then we'll be better placed to make an assessment of our future plans.

"In the meantime, Clive, please keep your spirits up for another three or four days and we promise to keep you informed. By the way, did you hear about the Irishman who couldn't tell the difference between his two horses? His friend suggested measuring them, but that didn't help as the Irishman discovered that the brown horse was only an inch taller than the white one! Ha! Ha!"

We left Clive in a fit of laughter and looking slightly happier than when we'd found him and headed back to Champs.

"Well, my Lord, when we get back to Champs, I need time on my own to do some more serious thinking and then we can decide together any further course of action."

I left Bigsby in the hotel lounge, with a bottle of Burgundy, while I retired to my room to attempt to evaluate our investigation to date. I now had an idea who the murderer was but I needed much more proof.

After speaking with Clive, and being implored to locate his missing horses, it was becoming more and more apparent that the head of a major crime organization was controlling the illegal activities at Campan.

After pondering the matter for a couple of hours, I rejoined Bigsby in the lounge.

"My dear Lord Bigsby, according to my rational way of thinking we have two options. We can go back to London tomorrow to see if we can uncover more information. There are a number of people I need to speak with from whom I need vital information.

"On the other hand, we have the dangerous option of uncovering the abductor of Clive's horses, hence discovering the real head of crime at Campan. This will allow us to bring together all the whys and wherefores of which we are not yet fully aware and so bring our task to a full conclusion. The latter option will be the more rewarding but we could be putting our lives at risk."

"We have put our lives at risk many times in the army, James, so we'll be more adept at coping with the situation than most other detectives, so let's go with the latter option."

"I totally agree with you, Bigsby, but we'll first need the assistance of Couture in relation to who he advises our first point of contact should be. If we are putting our lives at risk, we'll have a gourmet feast tonight with the finest of wine. The food tastes so much better, James, when someone else is paying for it."

"I'm having the seafood platter tonight as it includes winkles from the shores of Northern Scotland. The chef called it plateau de fruits de mer. He reliably informed me that the flavour and texture of this wonderful little mollusc is far superior to that of clams and oysters. A bottle of chardonnay will enhance the flavours nicely. Do you not agree, James?"

"You are the wine connoisseur, my Lord, and I will abide by what you advise. Couture will be calling to see us in the morning and he will hopefully accompany us to Campan to search for the registration documents of the horses. I also will have the seafood platter with a couple of extra oysters instead of the winkles. They remind me too much of the garden snail they call escargots to which they are related."

Bigsby enthused over the winkles but failed to tempt me into tasting one. I have never experienced such a fine fish dish anywhere. The following morning, Bigsby was late for breakfast which was so unusual for him. I went to his room to find out why. What a state he was in when I found him!

"Please give me something to calm my stomach, James. As soon as I reached the bedroom last night my dinner came up the same way as it went down. Never again am I having winkles! No breakfast for me this morning as I feel so awful!"

"Just imagine, Bigsby, those free range eggs, sausages and black puddings you'll be missing."

"Shut up, James! Get me something to ease my stomach pains."

"Very well, Bigsby. I'll ask that a cup of tea and a couple of aspirins be brought up to your room as soon as possible."

An hour later, after I'd eaten an excellent breakfast, Bigsby made an appearance in the lounge and he was feeling much better and in a happier frame of mind. We waited until Couture arrived but unfortunately he was unable to come with us because of other pressing matters he had to see to. He did give us an official signed paper to say we had his authority to act as we seemed fit.

For advice on how to proceed with the investigation into the whereabouts of Clive's horses, he advised us to call on the offices of the Haras Nationaux in Paris which was the administrative body responsible for the regulation and breeding of horses in France.

We then made our way to Campan to see if we could find the registration papers of the horses. We were in no doubt that they'd have been taken, as this was the only way to prove the authenticity of the thoroughbreds. We were certain, though, that the copies would still be in the safe in the wardrobe of Clive's home.

"Let's look in Clive's office first to see if the papers are there, James, but I'm guessing all the transactions relating to the purchases and sales of the horses will have also been taken."

"I'm sure you'll be correct, Bigsby. Goodness me! What a mess! Papers strewn everywhere! It looks like an expert has gone through everything with a fine toothcomb. No point in wasting time here; let's now make our way to Clive's house."

Clive's house was locked but with Bigsby's skill as a locksmith, which he'd picked up during his non-studies at Oxford, we were soon inside.

"Nothing appears to have been disturbed here, James, so it looks as though we'll be in luck. We'll go to his bedroom and look for the safe in his wardrobe. Hey, he keeps his house spotless with nothing out of place! No way can he have been in the Army!"

We eventually found the safe in the wardrobe as Clive had told us and once again the expertise of Bigsby in opening locks came in very handy. All the registration papers of the horses as well as Clive's written notes which included the races they had been entered for and their placings were there. At the bottom of the safe was a book in which the history of each horse and the progress they had made while under Clive's supervision at Campan, was listed and also four or five photographs of each horse. Clive did indeed love his animals and I was sure his superb photos would make them easier to identify.

CHAPTER THIRTEEN

"It's still quite early in the morning, my Lord, so let's begin our journey to Paris. It's a long journey so we'll have to stay somewhere overnight."

"Is Cognac in a direct route to Paris, James?"

"It certainly is, Bigsby—if you go in a kind of a roundabout way. By the name of the town, I don't have to guess your reason for desiring to go."

"I've heard so much about the Cognac house of Bache Gabrielsen that I'd very much like to visit it. It's situated in the centre of the town of Cognac. Did you learn anything about the history of the town in your studies at Cambridge, James?"

"I know it's situated on the River Charente and that Francis 1st was born in the castle there in 1494. I'm sure this information will be of great interest to you, Bigsby!"

"What senseless facts you can recall, James! I know very little about the distillation of brandy, but I'm extremely interested in learning about the process."

"You know plenty about drinking it, my Lord, and I know you're hoping for a free tasting. We'll begin our journey immediately as it's about two hundred and fifty miles to Cognac."

We had a wonderful drive as there was very little traffic and the sun was shining. We stopped at a small pavement café for a light lunch on the way. The first hotel we came to on the outskirts of Cognac was an elegant old chateau which really appealed to us both. We were by this time both very hungry so we decided to stay the night there.

"Our first priority is dinner, James, and by the look of the wine list it's a superb establishment."

"Goodness me, Bigsby. Do you know what the speciality of the day is? Seafood platter with winkles and white wine sauce!"

"Enough of that sarcasm, James! I'm keeping to the tried and trusted in future and tonight I'm having wagyu beef, roasted in white wine with chanterelles and truffles. It sounds delicious."

"I will join you, Bigsby, in having the same."

What a meal it was! I'm sure we'd chosen the best hotel in the area to stay. After relaxing in the lounge for a couple of hours, we retired to bed. The next morning, Bigsby could barely wait for our tour of the brandy distillery.

When we arrived at the distillery, we were warmly greeted by the tour guide who told us that the cognac house of Bache Gabrielsen was founded by Thomas Gabrielsen in 1905 and that it's still owned by the same family.

Our guide, Marie, informed us that she'd relate all the main points in connection to the creation of brandy while showing us around.

"Only green grapes are used in the production of brandy with Ugri Blanc the most common variety used. This grape is excellent in the distillation process as it's low in alcohol and high on acidity. We call the device we use for distillation an 'alambic Chatentais'. Cognac is distilled twice and the final product must contain at least 40% alcohol. The distilled product is then stored in oak casks to become cognac.

"Here's a leaflet for you to take which explains all the technical aspects of producing this fine spirit.

Now come and taste the final products as we have a variety to suit every palate and then you'll both receive a small bottle as a souvenir. It's very important to drink cognac out of tulip-shaped bottles as this traps the aroma much better than a normal glass."

Bigsby's face lit up like a child's when presented with the souvenir bottle. He also purchased a bottle for our own consumption, but I was sure it's contents wouldn't stay in the bottle for long. We both thanked Marie profusely for showing us around and then it was time for us to continue our trip to Paris.

"Oh, the joys of being a private detective and especially an amateur one, James. We're visiting wonderful places which we would otherwise not have done."

"Even an amateur detective, Bigsby, has to spend some time detecting, so let's make haste."

We arrived in Paris in the late afternoon and decided to stay the night at one of the smaller hotels. We only had a light meal as we were tired from driving, and then we went up to our rooms to sample the cognac. It suited perfectly the palates of both myself and Bigsby.

The following morning after breakfast, we started off quite early to the offices of the Haras Nationaux. We were greeted politely by the receptionist who enquired the reason for our visit and we were soon ushered into the offices of Sir Pierre Fille, a senior manager.

"Welcome to Paris, Lord Bigsby and Field Marshal James. I understand you've come to seek advice on discovering the whereabouts of a number of thoroughbred horses belonging to Sir Clive Ponywood which the late Lord Percy previously had a half share in. Could you please enlighten me a little further in connection to the circumstances of their disappearance and I'll do everything in my power to help?"

"Thank you most kindly, Sir Pierre. My friend, James, will proceed to give you the information you desire."

"Sir Percy, the acclaimed artist, bought the Campan Estate in southern France a number of years ago where he allowed his friend, Sir Clive Ponywood, a highly skilled veterinary surgeon specializing in the care of racehorses, to breed and train thoroughbred horses. This was a joint venture between the two friends. Unfortunately, for reasons unconnected with the dealings of the estate, Sir Percy was murdered and people with illegal tendencies were attempting to take over the estate.

"The opium factory we uncovered at the estate is no longer in production but we're thinking that there may be someone behind these illegal operations who is big time.

"Clive told us he was led to believe that his beloved horses, which he gave so much care and attention to, had been sold but it was his impression that they'd been abducted by the new owner of Campan. I'm sure this was pre-planned as these pedigree horses must be now worth hundreds of thousands of pounds, if not millions. We have in our possession the registration details and photographs of all the horses which were taken," I concluded.

"We're well aware of this problem, James," said Sir Pierre. "It infrequently happens but when it does it's the most valuable horses which are targeted. We're of the opinion that these criminals take the horses to unscrupulous trainers and breeders in either Spain or Portugal or own large stables themselves. Be very careful in your investigation as these are dangerous men and will not hesitate for one second to kill."

"Is there any help or advice you're willing to give us to proceed with our enquiries?" I asked.

"The second most important race meeting in France commences tomorrow at Chantilly racecourse," he replied. "All the leading trainers, breeders and owners will be in attendance, with a number of owners looking for quality horses to add to their stables. The best way for you to proceed is to go to Chantilly tomorrow and ask for Claude Fole who's highly regarded in the equestrian world. Also, ensure that General Couture meets you there tomorrow. If you're serious in your investigation, you'll need police protection. The best of good fortune to you both."

We thanked Sir Pierre for his help and left to find a reasonable-looking restaurant where we could have a hearty lunch. The gourmet meal we would partake of in the early evening.

"Seeing that you had your way in looking around a cognac distillery yesterday, I'd enjoy a visit to the Pantheon this afternoon. It's only thirty miles from Paris to Chantilly so we'll have plenty of time to find a decent hotel a little nearer to the racecourse."

We lunched at a small, typically French, café nearby where we both ordered the cassoulet which included pork sausages, salted pork, duck, goose and white beans. It was certainly filling and we would have been quite happy to stay there for an hour or two as we were fascinated with the Parisian lifestyle.

Eventually, we made our way to the Pantheon which was an early exemplification of neoclassicism with the building, originally a church, being dedicated to St. Genevieve. The exterior of the building reminded me very much of the Pantheon at Rome.

"What magnificent architecture, Bigsby."

"If only it had been a chateau, James, where wine was maturing in the barrel and surrounded on every side by acres of vineyards!"

Neither of us had any inclination to visit the Eiffel Tower on the Champ de Mars, so we headed in the direction of Chantilly to find accommodation for the night. With the races starting the following day, everywhere was very busy but we were eventually able to find two small rooms where we could spend the night.

No gourmet food here! The food was definitely not up to our standards by any stretch of the imagination, so we ordered a couple of plates of beef sandwiches to keep us going. What a disappointment! We decided to forego breakfast and made an early start to the racecourse.

Overlooked by the fairytale Chateau of Chantilly, it certainly was a majestic view that confronted us as we approached the racecourse. It adjoined the imposing building of the Great Stables, built in 1719, for the estate of the Princes de Conde. These were the longest stables in Europe and considered by many the most beautiful in the world. With the forest of Chantilly beyond, it was indeed a unique sight.

We went immediately to the grandstand where people were beginning to congregate, to ask the way to the office of Claude Fole. We were told the direction to go and soon found his room where he was sitting with his eyes closed, deep in thought, and a very worried expression on his face. We startled him as we knocked softly on the door to gain his attention.

"We're very sorry to disturb you, Mr. Fole, but we've been advised by Sir Pierre Fille to come to you with a problem we have about the kidnapping of racehorses belonging to our friend, Sir Clive Ponywood."

"Sir Clive, my goodness! We haven't heard anything about him for months. What a wonderful fellow and the greatest equestrian vet that I know! If Clive has problems then you have my full attention, notwithstanding the busy few days I have ahead."

We explained to Claude Fole what the situation was and it was decided to wait until the arrival of Couture who was expected at the racecourse shortly before lunch. Fole then led us into a small private room adjacent to his office and advised us to lock the door and stay out of sight for our own safety.

"Did you hear, Bigsby, about the tipster who backed his horse at ten to one and said it would walk it? It did, but all the others galloped!"

"Very similar to the person who told his friend that he'd put fifty pounds on a horse which had come in at twenty-five to one. 'Wow,' his friend said, 'that was a good win for you.' 'Not really,' he said, 'the rest of the field came in at twelve-thirty!'"

We then waited in silence for an hour before Claude returned accompanied by Couture, who was the first to speak.

"I've been speaking briefly with Claude here and we feel that we have to warn you that if you're both determined to continue your investigation into the disappearance of Clive's horses, that you'll be risking your lives. You'll be dealing with a ruthless person who's a criminal mastermind. Do you understand?"

"We most certainly do," said Bigsby. "For the sake of Lord Percy and Sir Clive who spent so much money on building up one of the best horse training and breeding stables in Europe, and especially for Clive who gave his precious racehorses so much love and care, we're prepared to take that risk.

"We're hoping that with our very amateurish way of detecting, they may greatly underestimate our ability and we'll be able to catch them off guard. If this is so, we'll have a much greater chance of success and, hopefully, come through unscathed."

"Have you anything to add, James?" asked Couture.

"I now have a thought who murdered Lord Percy and for what reason, but as yet I have no proof either way. I'm also under the impression that the present owner of Campan is the head of a criminal organization. It was only when Clive asked us to investigate the disappearance of his horses that I became certain in my own mind, that if we were successful, we would uncover his true identity."

"Well," said Couture, "if you're happy to go ahead, we'll begin immediately to make plans. Be aware that you'll have to go unarmed. If you're found carrying weapons, you'll be disposed of without ceremony and that'll be the end of you both. A sobering thought for two aristocrats who enjoy their fine wine!"

It was a sobering thought, indeed but we'd spent many years in the Army and therefore felt well enough equipped for what lay ahead.

"Well, Bigsby and James, I've been speaking with my colleagues this morning and we're all of one opinion. Our suspicions of Baron Gelding began two years ago. Previous to this, the Baron entered his horses in a few of the minor races at Chantilly and Longchamp but only occasionally did he saddle any winners.

"Two years ago, he entered horses for the classic races and did very well. Last year, he saddled a winner both in the Prix de l'Arc de Triomphe at Longchamp and the Prix du Jockey Club at Chantilly.

"As Baron Gelding had proper documentation for these horses, there was nothing we could do about it. He maintained that he'd purchased these horses from Australia. Could the documentations have been forged? If so, they were expertly done. We were aware that Clive no longer had horses, but there was nothing to suggest that these were his.

"Some of the other horses that had previously been unplaced in minor races were now winning higher class races. This also led to many of us raising more than an eyebrow.

"We were sure that narcotics must have been used to enhance their performance. Poor horses do not become winners overnight. We in the Jockey Club are resolutely against this, as drugs can adversely affect a horse's health. When pain and tiredness in the horse are masked by drugs, it can cause lasting damage to the horse's health.

"We have no method, as yet, that allows us to find out if illegal drugs have been used on the horses. We have no proof that the Baron is acting illegally. Until we get proof, we are unable to act.

"We in the horse racing fraternity are reasonably sure this is the place where the horses will be found. We know that the owner, whom we believe to be of English origin but who has been living in Spain or

Portugal for many years, goes by the name of Baron Gelding.

"Any owners who have ever wished to purchase a racehorse from the Baron are taken in a car where they are unable to see out of the windows, with armed guards accompanying them and under the strictest security. Once there, they're only able to view the animals they're interested in. Once the transaction is completed, they are immediately brought back. Please be absolutely certain you're willing to take the risk, as any error on your part will mean immediate death."

"Yes, we're willing, Claude," Bigsby and I said in unison, but I was sure that Bigsby's voice, like my own, contained more than a few trembles.

"If you're both sure, then I'll outline my plan for you which will have to be carried out an hour before the big race today which is scheduled for three o'clock.

"You, Lord Bigsby, will pose as an eccentric owner of thoroughbred racehorses who is desperately seeking new bloodstock of the highest quality to add to your stables. You will go under the name of the Earl of Fetlock and act in the peculiarly aristocratic way you high class British do. You will only need to display a little knowledge of the subject as James will be your professional advisor."

"Me!" I exclaimed in utter amazement. I play polo but I know very little about horses, only that they have four legs and most can run fast! Baron Gelding will be suspicious within two seconds!"

"Don't worry, James. As I'll give you a thorough briefing on everything to look for in regards to the horse's health and potential to win the big races. It'll take about two hours to go over all that you need to know so it's imperative to begin straight away.

"By the way, do you speak Spanish? The handlers who'll show you the horses which are available for sale, who are also armed guards, only speak their own language."

"Yes, Claude, I'm fluent in the Spanish language. Bigsby, though, can only speak his own peculiar brand of aristocratic English. Please make sure I'm in no danger of the powerful hind hoofs of these animals as I don't wish to be handicapped by broken bones!"

Claude led me outside to one of the private stables for my quick course of racehorse anatomy.

"Look to see if the horse seems physically strong and athletic looking and appears ready for action, and that everything about the horse is in proportion. Don't forget that all the power of a racehorse comes from its back legs, so make absolutely certain you examine the feet and ankle bones. Make sure the eyes look bright and alert and the nostrils are large.

"When you see the horse exercising, James, look at it from every angle and make certain it has an even and effortless gait. The height of a racehorse should be more or less sixteen hands with its large and heavy heart averaging ten pounds."

I had two hours of instruction like this on how to feel various parts of the animal to make sure all the required essentials were there. I wasn't sure how much knowledge I was gaining as many times I was getting confused.

I could see Bigsby out of the corner of my eye grinning at me all the time. After going through all I needed to know a few more times, Claude thought I had sufficient basic knowledge, but it was all time would allow. It was now back to planning our escapade.

We followed Claude back to his office where he outlined his plan for us.

"You and Bigsby will take a stroll around the stable and paddock areas with the intention of scrutinizing the horses and looking with greater interest at those that James appears to recommend to you. You'll be in deep conversation with each other as if you're prospective buyers.

"Eventually you'll approach the five owners separately, which I'll advise you of, and James will ask about any suitable horses, if any, they have for sale. You'll explain that the Earl of Fetlock is looking for horses, with potential to win big races, which he can add to his stable and that you're his advisor. Bigsby can still refer to you as James as there are many of that name connected to the horse racing world."

In twenty minutes, it would be time for us to go. Claude and his acquaintances were still unsure that any illegal activities were being carried out by Baron Gelding. Many were very suspicious that he was the head of a crime gang, but no one, including the police, had been able to bring any proof.

We were still arguing the case that we shouldn't go unarmed, but we finally accepted Claude's argument. If only we had judo and karate skills like our friend, Jacques, we would have felt a lot more secure. All we had going for us was our peculiarly aristocratic amateur detective skills!

"A horse with sixteen hands, I heard Jacques say! Had he been drinking, James?"

"My dear Lord Bigsby! You're supposedly the owner of a number of racehorses and yet you don't know that a horse's height is measured in hands!

Look alert and interested when walking around the stable and paddock areas, but I suggest you say as little as possible!"

When we reached the stables, many of the racehorses were still being housed. The owners were congregating around so I began pointing out to Bigsby the pros and cons of each horse we saw. I took out a notepad and made notes and sketches as I had been told to by Claude. I could again see the look of amusement in Bigsby's eyes even though he was trying very hard to remain serious looking.

After we'd walked around for nearly an hour, we began approaching the owners and asking about possible purchases. Only two had horses for sale which had already won races. One of these was our target Baron Gelding. After having a conversation with Bigsby and re-examining my notes, we approached the Baron.

"Good morning, sir," I said. "My eccentric and aristocratic friend, the Earl of Fetlock, wishes to add to his small stables in England by purchasing a thoroughbred racehorse with a proven track record. He also wishes to obtain a promising young horse with the potential to go on and achieve great victories.

"We've been examining a number of horses this morning, and we've come to the conclusion that there are two owners here whose horses have the superior qualities that my friend desires. It would be a great honour if you could help us in our search."

"Certainly I can help. I do have one horse at the moment, with a proven track record, which I have reluctantly decided to sell as my ambition now is to buy and breed younger horses where I can perceive that they have the ability to excel. Two of those that I bought recently aren't progressing as rapidly as I was expecting, but the potential is there for all to see if they receive attention from a first-class trainer.

"My trainers will take you to inspect the horses, where you'll be able to see them being exercised, if you so wish. My main stables are in Spain, where I live, but I've recently purchased another property in Belgium, where these horses are presently being trained."

"Thank you so much, Baron, for all your help. I'm sure my friend is more than interested, but I promised the other owner that I would also speak to him to see what he has to offer. I'll then have a conversation with the Earl to advise him on the course of action that I'd recommend him to take. We'll revert back to you shortly."

On speaking to the other owner, we found that he only had to offer second rate horses which did have a chance, but only a slight one, of improvement. I then had a chat with Bigsby, hoping it looked as though we were having a serious discussion, before we made our way back to speak with Baron Gelding.

"Good afternoon again, Baron Gelding. You're the only owner who's able to satisfy the demands of my client, the Earl of Fetlock, and we're very grateful for your generous offer of being able to inspect these horses. We're sure they'll be of the highest calibre as we are fully aware how many of the classic races your stable has won."

"It's a pleasure for me to be able to assist the Earl and to have the knowledge that the horses will be in the safest of hands if he does indeed decide to purchase them. They come highly recommended by myself.

"Two of my trainers will accompany you to the stables in Belgium in thirty minutes, and then I myself will follow in three hours. Do either of you speak Spanish as that's the only language my two employees speak."

"I speak a little Spanish," I replied. "Hopefully, it'll be adequate to converse with them. The Earl and I will now have a little refreshment in the racecourse café before we begin the journey."

The food in the café was of the greasy variety and repulsive to ourselves, so we contented ourselves with a cup of coffee and Belgian waffles.

"I remember a Belgian joke, James, that I was told years ago, about a Belgian who drowned. He threw his cigarette into the sea and then jumped after it because he'd forgotten to put it out!! Ha! Ha!"

A little humour relaxed us, but we did try to appear that we were seriously concentrating on horse talk.

CHAPTER FOURTEEN

It was not long before the Baron's trainers came and ushered us to a Rolls Royce parked nearby.

We were asked to sit in the back seat of the car where a small bar with bottles of spirits was easily accessible but, unfortunately for Bigsby, no red wine. The seats were luxuriously upholstered but there were blinds on the windows and a partition between ourselves and the driver so we were unable to see which direction we were heading. We'd been travelling for two and a half hours before the car pulled to a halt and the driver, Carlos, pulled back the partition to speak to us.

"We've arrived at our destination, Earl Fetlock, and as you'll see, this yard is the most modern with the best health and training facilities in the world. We frequently take in injured racehorses which have been cruelly discarded by other owners and patiently bring them back to fitness. Some have made it back to the racecourse and have done exceptionally well. My friend, Marcos, will now open the gates to allow you to view the horses you've expressed interest in purchasing. I know you'll be more than pleasantly surprised."

I watched very closely the way that Marcos unlocked the gates in case we had need of a rapid escape from danger later in the day but it appeared a simple locking mechanism. I was expecting Bigsby to have been interested also, but he appeared totally unconcerned and was looking in the opposite direction.

"The horses in which you're interested are in adjoining stables, so we'll drive you the short distance there to enable you to inspect them thoroughly. Please take your time as we don't want you to be disappointed in their capabilities. Afterwards, I'll ride them around our training circuit for you both to watch them in action," said Marcos.

"Thank you so much for this," I said.

It only took a couple of minutes to reach the stables where I was utterly stunned. If Marcos and Carlos hadn't been fully occupied with saddling the horse, they would've been immediately aware of our intention as our demeanour momentarily changed drastically.

I was shaking and totally speechless. I felt as if I'd been hit by a thunderbolt! This was truly one of Clive's precious horses as there was no mistaking it from the photographs I'd examined so minutely. Finally, after the initial shock, I was able to speak.

"I know a superb horse as soon as I see one, which is a very rare experience. Everything about the looks of this horse speaks class. Could I please examine this wonderful beast more closely?"

"Ciertamente, mi señor. I will lead 'Steal A Treat' outside where the sun is shining."

I examined everything Claude had instructed me to, but I couldn't find even the slightest fault. The gait was superbly athletic, ears pricked and ready for action. Marcos rode the horse around the circuit a few times, but I already knew its qualities. Even without the knowledge I'd been given earlier in the day, I knew 'Steal A Treat' was in a class of its own.

I then had a quiet word with Bigsby out of earshot of the others, but I was asking him what we would be having for dinner that evening and the wine he would be choosing if we had the good fortune to survive our experience here! Poor Bigsby hadn't been able to understand a word of what was being said as everything had been spoken in Spanish and I could feel the tension building up inside him.

Out of the two novice horses, neither appeared good enough to win races at the present, but I did think one of them, if patiently brought on and well trained, could become a high class racehorse, so this was the one I chose. I couldn't believe the knowledge I'd learned from Claude in those two hours.

After another short conversation with Bigsby, I approached the two trainers to tell them our decision. We were then invited indoors to wait in the ornately constructed chateau for the arrival of the Baron.

"This is the most wonderful experience I've had in a long time. Never before have I seen accommodations for horses of such a high standard and I'm also thrilled that the Baron never forgets the horses that have been injured in races," I said.

"El baron es muy amable y generoso. Se preocupa mucho on los animals y personas," said Marcos.

At that moment, we heard a car drive up to the chateau and then heard a knock on the door. Both the trainers rose in unison to greet the new arrival.

The conversation they were having was in their own local Spanish dialect as they must have been sure that I wouldn't know a word of what was being said. Fortunately, I had studied Spanish as an extra subject while at Cambridge and had been most intrigued by the different dialects so I understood clearly.

I was beginning to panic as the visitor said that the Baron now had serious doubts about our objective and was making further enquiries and would deal with us in the appropriate manner as soon as he arrived back at his chateau.

I did have one trick up my sleeve that Bigsby was unaware of. I was sure he would, as he always did, play along with it and show no element of surprise.

"Well, my dear Earl Fetlock, our trip to Chantilly has certainly been a success," I said to Bigsby. "In a few hours, you'll be the owner of the finest racehorse in the world and another that's capable of emulating it. Let's drink to your success and the kindness of the Baron and our two friends here.

"While we were in Cognac the other day, I purchased eight small bottles of the finest brandy. I have only four left now which I have with me, so I propose a toast to Baron Gelding."

There was not the slightest flicker of emotion from Bigsby. Normally he'd be up in arms at the waste of such fine brandy to anyone, let alone a couple of men who we looked on as criminals.

"Here we are," I said, as I passed the bottles around. "Let's open the brandy and drink to the health of the Baron. Cheers, or shall I say, 'Salud' as I'm of the opinion that that is the Spanish equivalent."

I gulped the brandy down in one gulp with the others following suit. In a few minutes time, our two friends started laughing and singing with great gusto before they fell soundly asleep.

"Don't waste any time, Bigsby," I said. "There's plenty of rope in the corner over there so I'll tie them up securely and put them somewhere in one of the rooms at the back of the chateau where they won't be easily found. You utilize your expertise of opening the safe and then we'll gather what appears to be the most important papers and take them with us. Hopefully, we may gain more knowledge of who the Baron really is."

"I've opened the safe now, James, so I'll get the Rolls started and open the gate and wait for you there."

After I'd tied the two trainers securely and taken a number of documents from the safe, I went to join Bigsby. He already had the gate open and was waiting in the driver's seat.

"It would have been a very difficult lock to open if I hadn't been fully concentrating on the mechanism when Marcos opened it. It was very similar to the lock on the entrance to the shooting range at Oxford which I've opened many times without a key. It wasn't the key turning that you should have had your eyes on, James, it was how the locking mechanism worked. By the way, what happened to our two friends?"

"I knew there was a possibility that we might be in danger at some time and, being armed would arouse suspicion. While I was looking in the window of one of the wine shops in Cognac, my eyes fell upon a bottle of Spiritus Delikatesowy. As you are well aware, it's a ninety-five per cent proof vodka from Poland, and I bought a large bottle.

"When we arrived in Paris, I filled two small empty brandy bottles with the vodka for distribution to any enemies we might encounter and filled two empty bottles with water for ourselves to drink. You did very well not to show any surprise at all when you drank it, Bigsby. My amateur detective brain was of the opinion that a criminal's weakness was the consumption of alcohol."

"It's time to think about our present predicament now, James, and how we reach a main road without being caught."

"Don't you remember, Bigsby, that we spent many months in Belgium during the years we were in the Army and marched for miles during training exercises."

"Look, James, that old watermill on our left. Surely you remember the night we spent there with those two gorgeous young ladies. It was our first posting abroad after we'd joined the Army.

"Those were the days, James, my lad. When the Commander found out he told us if it happened again we'd be court martialled and shot. The measly scoundrel! He only found out because it was the place he'd arranged to stay that night with his own lady-love and saw us!"

"You're right, Bigsby! I remember the architecture—like those two shapely ladies—was something wondrous to behold. It means we're only four miles from Charleroi.

"There were so many cul-de-sacs around that made our training marches difficult, but I'll never forget the way to Charleroi from here. Well spotted, my dear Lord."

Another ten minutes and we were on the outskirts of the city, where we asked the way to the nearest police station. On arrival, we asked if they would contact General Couture at Chantilly racecourse where he'd be expecting our call as it was of the utmost urgency.

After a quarter of an hour, we were put through and I could hear the relief in his voice.

"Excellent to know you're both safe. The more Claude and I thought about your mission, the more dangerous it appeared to be. Please tell me briefly what occurred and I'll arrange assistance without delay."

I related briefly to Couture the situation, and that the Baron would be arriving at his chateau later that afternoon and would be immediately concerned by both the absence of the Rolls and the non-appearance of his two trainers.

After a few minutes thought, Couture said he'd dispatch instructions to his friends in the Belgian police at Charleroi and direct them to the police station, where we were enquiring from, without delay. He, himself, would immediately make all speed to Charleroi.

Baron Gelding, he knew, was still at Chantilly as he could see him in the winner's enclosure congratulating his horse and jockey who a few moments previously had won the big race of the day.

The Belgian police were soon with us and we explained the situation to them also. As Couture would be arriving at Charleroi before the Baron, it was decided to await his arrival before any action was taken. We waited in near silence with the police offering us light refreshments. Eventually, he arrived and greeted us with great emotion.

"That was superb work, Bigsby and James," said Couture. "To incapacitate the two trainers without violence and for Bigsby to understand the mechanism involved to open the gate is amazing. I'm so proud of you both.

"We'll now go to a vantage point where we'll be able to watch for Baron Gelding returning to his stables from Chantilly. A couple of minutes later, we'll follow with your guidance and, hopefully, there won't have been enough time for the gate to be opened. He will be trapped! The Belgian police will follow immediately behind us."

We went with Couture and the chief of the Charleroi police to the vantage point and, after a fifty minute wait, the Baron, in a chauffeur-driven Rolls, passed by. When they were out of sight, we followed. As we'd marched around this area so many times during the war, it brought back many memories.

We didn't see the Rolls again until we reached the gate that Bigsby had so expertly unlocked. The chauffer was in the process of opening it when we drew up, with the sirens on all the police cars blaring away.

"He'll make no attempt to escape or use firearms while we're here, but will give himself up peacefully," said Couture. He knows the game's up for the present and will be imprisoned, but he also knows that in a few weeks, his associates will have devised a plan for his escape. After his escape, he will gain a new identity and once again resume his role as mastermind of his criminal empire."

The Baron got out of his car and came over to us to congratulate us on his capture, but then he spoke with excitement about the race meeting at Chantilly and how well his horses had performed. Couture invited him to get in the police car where he was handcuffed, all the while chatting away unconcernedly about his belief that he would soon be a free man again.

I was in no way surprised when I saw his appearance as there was no mistaking who he was. After living in Portugal for many years, with his tanned appearance, he now looked more like a local than an English man. Everything concerning the death of Lord Percy, in my mind, had now fallen entirely into place.

One of the local police cars stayed behind to apprehend the two trainers and to await the arrival of the serious crime squad.

Back at the police station, we took Couture's advice on a choice of hotel to accommodate us for the night and invited him for a meal to converse about old times and all the exploits we'd shared together. Before we left, we examined the documents we'd taken from the Baron's safe but there was no incriminating evidence.

"We deserve a special meal tonight, my Lord, or do I call you the Earl of Fetlock?" I said. "We'll dine on the most expensive fare and drink the finest wine on offer. I'm sure the Belgian and the Spanish police will be more than willing to foot the bill! I can't wait to partake of the confit de canard. I love duck whatever way it's cooked, but cooking it slowly in its own fat must be delicious."

"I, myself, will be only too happy to pay for the meal," said Couture. "We've been trying to find enough proof to arrest this man for over twenty years, and you two manage to do it with the help of Polish spirit. Who would believe it!"

"Do you have any spiritus delikatesowy left, James? I'm sure Couture would enjoy a glass!"

"After I'd seen the effect of it on our two trainer friends, I thought it wise to empty the remains of the bottle down the toilet!"

"I'll sample the Paling in't groen, as I've never eaten eel before. I'll try anything after the experience we've been through today," said Bigsby.

Couture also decided on the eel menu, but hoped the proprietor didn't think he was a slippery customer! They were both rather dubious about ordering eel, but it turned out to be a superb meal, as was also the duck.

After the meal, we retired early to bed as we had a long drive back to Lourdes which we decided to take over three days. We passed through Orleans, Limoges and Toulouse before reaching Lourdes. If only there had been time, we could have made it a wonderful adventure. We were so glad to be back at Champs as the tension of the last few days hadn't yet worn off.

"Tomorrow, Bigsby, we'll have a stroll around the vineyard here at Champs, take in the invigorating fresh air and completely relax."

"Do you still not comprehend the fact, James, that one is unable to relax without a glass of wine by their side?"

"This is surely not a problem, Bigsby, when we have some of the finest wine produced in France readily available on the premises."

"No problem at all, James, when all our expenses are being paid in full by Lady Helen. How much did you say that fine bottle of claret cost?"

"You haven't told me yet what the two visitors to the Baron's chateau said, James."

"They were saying that Baron Gelding had become very suspicious of us because we were totally unknown to any of the other owners he'd spoken to afterwards and he was making further enquiries. The Baron had given orders for Marcos and Carlos to keep us very secure and in no circumstances to let us escape until he arrived.

"I thought then it was time to put my little plan into action. You played along with it wonderfully, Bigsby, as I fully expected you to. You must have had a little surprise when you tasted water instead of cognac!"

"To think, James, that the police would have surrounded a criminal mastermind's estate with armed men to attempt to capture him which would, more than possibly, have ended with bloodshed and killings. All two Oxbridge educated graduates turned amateur detectives needed was a little ingenuity and strong alcohol to perform the same task peacefully. How foolish must Marcos and Carlos feel!"

We spent the remainder of the day relaxing in the vineyard before dining early.

"Are there any details you still need to check here in France?" asked Bigsby after our meal.

"As I said before, my Lord, I do have my suspicion as to the killer of Lord Percy. Something has been nagging at the back of my mind for the last few days. I was sure this was vital to our investigation. Last night, I suddenly remembered what it was. To be sure of its importance I need to visit Lourdes tomorrow before we go back to London."

At breakfast the following morning, I asked Bigsby if he'd arrange for our travel back to London while I took a quick trip into Lourdes.

"Who do you have in mind as to who you think the killer is, James? Everything, to my mind, is still so confused. I still think the murderer is Sir Clive, however contrite he appeared yesterday."

"If you'd been educated at Cambridge, like myself, and gained an enquiring, academic mind, you also would have some idea by now!"

"Enough cheek, James! Don't forget how thankful you were when Sir Clive started shooting at us. Much more useful spending time on the shooting range than in the lecture hall!"

On my visit to Lourdes, I wandered around the town for a little while and then went to the orphanage where I spoke to the matron. I then revisited the home of Dax where I found everything as it had been a few days previously. I then made my way back to Champs.

"We'll miss the fresh, pure air of the Pyrenees, James. I'll be bringing my paints, canvas and easel with me if we ever return to the area."

Unless he had some hidden talent that I wasn't aware of, I'm sure his finished work would resemble, at best, a composition of clashing colours!

Couture arrived to wish us farewell.

"Au revoir, messieurs! I will informally question Baron Gelding tomorrow. I will pass on to you any information I think of importance that results from this."

Couture asked us to keep him informed of events which we promised to do. Then we were on our way back to London.

CHAPTER FIFTEEN

After arriving back in London, we spent the remainder of that day with our families and agreed to meet the next day at our office in The Club at nine o'clock. We both certainly needed time to relax for the day ahead.

We arrived early at the Club the following day where Bigsby asked me what I had planned for us both.

"Your task, my Lord, is to remain in the office and speak to no one until I come back. You must refrain from alcohol so as to keep your mind alert for this evening when we'll announce to Lady Helen and the family who was the murderer of Lord Percy and why he was murdered.

"I'm now going to get the final proof that I need. There's a number of people I have to speak to and a few duties to undertake. I'll update you with everything when I return this afternoon. We'll then have to think of the best possible way to inform Lady Helen and her family of the result of the investigation, at her home, this evening."

My first visit was to the Mayfair Memorial Hospital to enquire if the matron had returned from her holiday in America. Fortunately, she had and I asked if I could speak to her. I told her we were investigating the death of Lord Percy and I wanted to know if she could recall any of the conversation that had taken place between Lord Percy and the father of Carolee after the births of Priscilla and Carolee.

I no longer believed that Carolee was unaware who her father was. I was, therefore, happy with what was explained to me by the Matron. I was sure it was the truth. I now realized more fully what an upright and gracious man Lord Percy was. I had the deepest sympathy for him.

Now a trip to the London Law Courts for help on three counts was necessary. My first two requests were easily obtained. My third request was for details of a law case which had taken place a number of years earlier and to enquire if any other legal proceedings had taken place as a result of this.

During my appraisal of our investigation before we arrived back in London, I began to realize the significance of information we'd been given but not thought, at the time, how vital some of it was. I now realized it was of paramount importance to our enquiries. I was told by the staff at the Law Courts to return in a couple of hours when everything would be ready for me to collect. I thanked them and then carried on to my next destination.

At the Peregino Auction House, I was surprised when I was greeted by Neric Taraya.

"So nice to meet you again, Neric, but what brings you to London?" I asked.

"I'm here to gain practical knowledge of the day to day business of the Auction House and the work of an auctioneer and valuer. I will be the auctioneer at our next auction of fine art where some pieces are expected to bring very high prices. I'm so excited at the prospect."

"You appear to enjoy your work, Neric."

"The only downside, Field Marshal James, is that I'm confined to stuffy offices in the cities. I have always lived in the countryside and that's my first love. I really do hate towns and cities. My passion is walking in the mountains and the foothills of the Pyrenees where I can watch and photograph the wildlife and the wildflowers. If I was offered employment in the countryside today I'd accept without question."

"Lord Bigsby and I will invite you out for a meal tomorrow at The Club if you're free to come. We'll bring a beautiful young lady as a companion for you who's also a lover of the countryside," I said to Neric cheekily, at which he blushed.

"I'd love to come as very few of my friends hold the same interests as I do."

"Very good, Neric, and we'll look forward to it. What I have really come for is to ask if you have any paintings of the racehorses at Campan which were painted by Lord Percy. He possessed an amazing memory for detail and he could paint an exact likeness of either people or animals even hours after he'd seen them.

"If so, would you be able to keep them for a little while as Bigsby and I would dearly love, with the blessing of Lady Helen, to present Clive with an original painting of one of his favourite racehorses. After all the distress he's been through, he surely deserves something which he will cherish."

"Just one minute and I'll go and see."

Neric came back with two paintings by Lord Percy and he willingly agreed to keep them in a place of safe keeping for a few days. I wished him farewell and then carried on to my final call of the afternoon to collect the documents from the law courts. I now knew that we had the proof we needed to present to Lady Helen this evening that would reveal who killed her husband and why.

I then returned to our office at The Club to
explain to Bigsby my findings. Bigsby showed real
surprise when he heard from me who the murderer
was, but he agreed that with the evidence we'd
gained, there was no doubt at all. Bigsby then
contacted the police so they'd take the appropriate
action.

CHAPTER SIXTEEN

"Well, James, we have only to put the final touches to the case and then we can celebrate in style. We'll have our evening meal now before we visit Lady Helen and when we get back, we'll open a bottle of wine that Jacques and Pierre gave us from the Chamour vineyard."

After our meal, we went over our plans again in detail before we made our way to Lady Helen's. We were both a little nervous and filled with trepidation. Sir Martin opened the door and bade us enter. Everyone in the room looked very tense and anxious. We were motioned to sit in the two most comfortable armchairs which we refused.

Our plan was to stay standing near the person whom we expected the most reaction from so as to be ready for all eventualities. I informed them all that Sir Clive was now in prison at Montpellier. One could feel the tension in the room ease slightly after I'd told them this. Sir Martin was the first to react.

"That despicable person! If he were here right now I'd throttle him with my bare hands. If I get the chance I certainly will. How can anyone kill an honest and upright person like Lord Percy? Murderers should be hung, drawn and quartered and I'll give my blessing to this every time."

I then addressed Sir Martin. "Why, Sir Martin, after Lady Helen has shown you much love and kindness and helped you to acquire a cherished position with the internationally renowned auction

house of Peregrino International Auction Services,
did you abuse this affection and trust?"

"What do you mean, James? The auction house
has prospered due to my diligence and I've recently
been promoted to a directorship of the company."

I interrupted him. "Could you please allow me to
speak for a few minutes and explain, Sir Martin?

"Four years after you'd gained your doctorate
from Oxford, your father and Lord Harry, the father
of Lord Percy, entered into a joint business deal
which would've allowed both parties, in normal
circumstances, to have gained extreme wealth from.
But, unforeseen by the City and the financial
markets, the economy took a severe downturn.

"This meant that both parties lost all the
considerable amount of money they'd invested.
Lord Harry, because of his substantial wealth and
his many other investments, was able to ride the
storm, but your father was left all but bankrupt."

"Who told you all this rubbish or have you just
made it up for your own amusement, James?"

"Rubbish, indeed not, Sir Martin. Your father
then took Lord Harry to court in an attempt to
recover part of his lost capital on the pretext that
Lord Harry acted fraudulently in advising him to
invest in their joint business deal. As your father
lost the case, he had to pay his own legal fees and
also the cost of the hearing which drove him to
bankruptcy."

"How foolish can you get, James? Do you think I
murdered Lord Percy so as to gain revenge for my
late father?"

"Please let me continue. Three years previous to
this, your father had financed you with your wish to
purchase an auction house. You possessed great
theoretical knowledge of the art world, but you did

not have the practical ability to make a business succeed. With your father's financing you were able to employ an experienced and well respected auctioneer as your business advisor. Your auction house 'Martin's Fine Art Auctioneers and Valuers' expanded beyond anyone's belief and it was fast becoming one of the prime auction houses in London.

"Just as it was on the brink of becoming financially viable, disaster struck, and your father— now bankrupt—could no longer support you. You and your business advisor had worked so hard for three years and great success was at your fingertips. The business, without any more capital forthcoming, now faltered and all your labour had come to nothing. I really do feel for you. You must have been heartbroken and devastated beyond words."

"You're correct there, James. I very nearly lost my sanity and I was quickly becoming an alcoholic until I regained my senses. How did you find all this out?"

"We're private detectives, Sir Martin, and this is what you advised us to do. I was first put on the trail by Lord Percy's accountant and, coupled with your desire to exact money from Lord Percy, I checked with Companies House to see if your father was, in fact, the business partner of Lord Harry. Your desire for financial revenge was great."

"No-one knows how I suffered when I had to give up my dream. Another six months of finance and we'd have become highly respected, both at home and internationally, and financially very secure. All my hard work for nothing. There are no words to express how I felt. I no longer cared about anything and this eventually led me into thoughts of revenge. James, I'm far from being a murderer, but if I find out who killed Lord Percy, I could possibly become one."

The tension in the room was again beginning to mount and I could feel it would soon be out of control. I could see Bigsby sweating, with deep concentration etched on his face. I now confronted Carolee.

"Carolee, stand up," I said gently.

"Don't be stupid! How can I when I am disabled?"

The tension and anger was starting to build up inside me. I went closer to Carolee and hauled her out of her wheelchair.

"Stand up, you murderess," I said with real venom in my tone. This was the moment I'd been keeping alert for. Carolee was like lightening. She had her gun out in a flash, ready to kill her father. I was nearly taken off guard by her speed but I was able to twist her gun arm round away from everyone.

Before I could bend her arm any further, the gun fired. The bullet pierced her heart and Carolee, the killer of Lord Percy, the killer of her two male friends at Lourdes and the person who'd ordered the killing of Jacques and Pierre was dead.

Sir Martin was on his feet immediately. By the look of rage on his face, I'm certain he would've strangled Carolee if she'd not been already dead. Bigsby took hold of him and led him back to his seat. His apologies to Lady Helen that his daughter had killed her late husband were profuse and certainly genuine. The bitter hatred he now had for his daughter was clear for all to see.

The police, who we'd warned beforehand of the probability that Carolee might try to shoot her father, heard the shots and immediately came in to take Carolee's body away. Priscilla was sobbing loudly. Lady Helen eventually broke the silence.

"I'll go and make a cup of tea to calm us all down a little and then we'll allow James to continue to inform us of the results of the investigation."

After a cup of tea, I continued. There was a somber, eerie feel in the room as I spoke.

"This morning, Sir Martin, I obtained a court order to enable me to discover who was the father of Carolee from the Registrar. I wasn't surprised when I found out that you were her father.

Now I'll be as brief as possible, but I'll begin with Sir Martin's lust for financial revenge. Sir Martin's love affair with the wife of a prominent member of the House of Lords led to the birth of a daughter one day before Priscilla was born. Having heard that Lady Helen was due to give birth at the same hospital, he persuaded the staff to allow his daughter, because she was disabled, to remain at the hospital for a few extra days of special care.

Two weeks previous to this, Sir Martin had contacted his brother, Dr. Colin Nash, for advice on what action to take when the baby was born. He was aware that the mother would flee the hospital as soon as possible after the birth. His brother, who lived in Portugal, told him to take the baby to the orphanage at Lourdes where he'd ensure that she was well cared for as he lived not many miles away.

As soon as Martin knew that Lady Helen was being admitted to the hospital, he phoned his brother again. It was agreed between them to tell Lord Percy that he'd be responsible for the child until the age of eighteen as retribution for the way Lord Harry had treated their father.

Sir Martin then kept watch on the hospital for Lord Percy to arrive and followed him into the ward. Lady Helen was still being treated in intensive care because of the difficult birth so it was easy for him to begin an argument which resulted in Lord Percy being given the ultimatum as agreed with his brother.

Sir Martin also told him that if he didn't acquiesce to this demand, he'd contact all the newspaper editors in London so that the world would know how Sir Harry had behaved towards his father. He would also make sure he created the biggest scandal of all time. His other demand was that he should take Carolee to the orphanage at Lourdes where arrangements had already been made.

Sir Martin then left the hospital as neither he nor the mother had any interest in caring for the child. Lord Percy, the real gentleman that he was, told the matron, who'd overheard everything that had been spoken, of his decision to agree to this and be accountable for the upbringing of the child so as not to cause any further distress to anyone.

As luck would have it, the matron was travelling to France the following day to see her sister and she was very willing to take the baby with her. She would then travel to the orphanage in Lourdes and establish that it was up to the required standard where the infant would receive all the attention she required.

This was then agreed. The matron would accompany the baby to the orphanage and after that all the responsibility of financing her care would fall on Lord Percy. That baby girl was Carolee. I'm also sure that Sir Martin was happy with the financial and emotional revenge he'd gained and that he planned no further action against Lord Percy.

Priscilla then said in a weak voice, "I thought Carolee was my friend, but instead she must have despised me. But please continue, Field Marshal James."

"Nothing of any consequence to our investigation took place until about eight years later. While Lord Percy was on holiday in Sussex, he became very friendly with Sir Clive Ponywood, the noted veterinary surgeon, who specialized in the care of racehorses. Together they would visit the races.

"This whetted Lord Percy's appetite and on his next trip to Lourdes, he saw an advert announcing the sale of an agricultural and horse breeding estate only twenty miles away from the town. After making enquiries with the estate agents to ensure this was a viable business, he invited Sir Clive to join him in this enterprise. For Sir Clive it was a dream come true. Lord Percy went ahead and purchased the estate."

"Why didn't he inform me and Priscilla and then we could have enjoyed some wonderful holidays there? Both Priscilla and I would have loved the countryside and the mountains of the Pyrenees," said Lady Helen.

"When Carolee was fifteen, Lord Percy paid for her to enter the hospital at Montpellier for exploratory tests which indicated her paralysis was fully curable if she was willing to undergo a major operation. This she was more than willing to do and after the operation and a period of intense physiotherapy, she regained full mobility.

This was the time when Carolee began to scheme in earnest as she was now free of any physical restraint. She told Lord Percy that the operation had *not* been a success, and that she was still confined to her wheelchair, so he would continue to provide for her needs. She was always fully aware when Lord Percy's short visits would be so she could then returned to the orphanage and sit in her wheelchair while she painted.

"The reason, Lady Helen, that your husband produced more paintings when he began his annual trips to the Pyrenees was for Carolee's upkeep. You also informed me that he donated the proceeds of eighteen of his paintings each year to a children's charity in France.

"Sir Martin interrupted angrily, "Why are you spinning us this fantastic yarn, James? If you have any proof—which you don't appear to have—we may believe you."

I kept my cool as I responded, "Not long before his death, Lord Percy unexpectedly visited Lourdes on his way to Campan as he'd heard a rumour that there were illegal activities taking place on his estate.

"At Lourdes, he saw Carolee engaged in physical activity with no sign of paralysis in her legs. This worried Lord Percy and he began to plan revenge because the trust he'd placed in people had been broken. Unbeknownst to him, though, Carolee had also spotted him."

Lady Helen now spoke, "How did my husband try and gain revenge, Field Marshal James?"

"To put it briefly, Lady Helen, we were told that he was going to hire a private detective to look into the activities of Sir Clive. He died before he was able to do this.

"In Carolee's psychopathic mind, Lord Percy had to die because he would most likely have found out what illegal activities she'd planned for the Campan Estate. Revenge for her grandfather's bankruptcy was also a major factor in her decision. She visited your house here when he was alone and poisoned him."

"You said Carolee had murdered others. Who were they and why did she kill them?" asked Sir Martin.

"Her boyfriend, Dax, who she lived with and another friend found out too much about her activities. Priscilla would also have been murdered if we'd not taken her back to Champs with us.

"She also ordered the deaths of the two farm managers for the same reason, but the two guards from Campan who'd been tasked to kill them didn't know that one of them was an expert in martial arts. It was the guards who ended up in the grave that they'd dug for the farm managers!"

"Do you expect us to believe this, James?" said Sir Martin.

"Let me start from the first time you came to see us to ask us if we'd investigate the disappearance of Priscilla. You became our first suspect as we both realized that you had no affection for your wife or step-daughter and you were prone to lying. Your insistence that our investigations should only include the disappearance of Priscilla only strengthened our belief.

"Our second suspect was Sir Clive Ponywood for the reason that he'd always been in full-time employment at Campan and he was also involved in the drug smuggling.

"Our third suspect, or my third suspect, was Carolee. Bigsby wouldn't believe me as he saw Carolee as a disabled child who'd been deprived of a family upbringing. It was his great desire to bring her into the fold of Lady Helen's household where she'd have a close and loving friend in Priscilla."

"That's certainly correct, James," said Bigsby. "I was certainly taken in by her and I'll have to learn to trust no one, until proven otherwise, in any future cases we take on, but please continue."

"Lord Percy did all he could to help her under the circumstances, but her father deserted her, which deprived her of much needed paternal care.

"She must have spent her years consumed with her painting and her thoughts of revenge. Revenge for her grandfather's bankruptcy, revenge for desertion by her parents, revenge for her loneliness, revenge for her disability.

"Revenge must have obsessed her mind and turned her into a maniac. After her paralysis was cured, she saw it as the time to act.

"Our final suspect was Baron de Beuna, but, apart from being told that he gave orders at Campan, he remained a mystery."

"What led you to the killer and do you now know who Baron de Buena is, Field Marshal James?" asked Lady Helen.

"All in good time, Lady Helen. Bigsby and I stopped Sir Clive on the way to Marseilles to deliver heroin. Bigsby immobilized his car with a shot to his back tire which resulted in a blow-out.

"He was terrified beyond words as he was sure this was the work of Baron de Buena and he was about to be killed. As he'd fired warning shots, he was arrested and taken to the Montpellier police station where he was kept in a cell awaiting trial.

"We visited him a few days later to question him. He was a broken man. He was a zombie. No actor could have come close to acting a part like this. We realized then that Sir Clive was an honest and an upright man, but psychologically, when he lacked a trusted friend to turn to, he was very weak. Sir Clive was far from being a murderer."

"Carolee always told me how much she loved me and how wonderful it was to have a sister like me," whispered Priscilla.

"I'll come to that shortly, Priscilla," I said softly.

"I was sure there had been something far more sinister and dangerous taking place at Campan. It was Clive Ponywood who eventually enabled my mind to think in the correct direction. I doubted the ability of Carolee to begin a drug smuggling operation by herself as this requires a lot of knowledge. I was then convinced there was an unknown criminal mastermind that had been controlling operations there. *Was this Baron de Buena?* I asked myself, *and how could I uncover his identity?*

"It was when Clive pleaded with us to find the whereabouts of his racehorses which had been taken away from Campan, that I was sure, if we acquiesced to Clive's plea that in doing this would give us a chance of uncovering his true identity. I was advised by the police to visit the offices of the Haras Nationaux, in Paris, who would be able to advise us.

"Clive is a brilliant veterinary surgeon whom both Bigsby and I now have the greatest respect for but, unfortunately, he suffers from a severe personality disorder. Even though we knew this could be a very dangerous assignment, we agreed to take it on both for Clive's sake and also to bring our investigation into Lord Percy's death to an absolute conclusion.

"We made the journey to Paris where we were recommended to visit Chantilly racecourse and speak to Claude Fole, a well-respected follower of horseracing. He advised us that one major owner had been suspected of stealing racehorses for a long time, but the police had been unable to act as there was no proof forthcoming.

"With the help of Claude Fole and General Couture, our friend from the French police, we devised a plan to infiltrate the stables of the suspect, Baron Gelding. Bigsby was to act as an eccentric English racehorse owner who wished to add quality to his stables and I was his adviser.

"We spoke with the Baron about this and we agreed to visit his stables in Belgium and examine the horses, in view of a possible sale. We were taken there by two of his trainers where we were able to ascertain, from photographs that Clive had taken, that one horse we inspected was originally from Campan.

"We were then taken into the large chateau to await for the arrival of the Baron to discuss a possible purchase, but word was brought to the two trainers that we might be imposters and they were instructed to keep us hostages. Fortunately, I'm fluent in Spanish and unbeknownst to them, I understood what was said.

With a little ingenuity from me and with Bigsby's skill at opening locks, we were able to escape and inform General Couture via the Belgian police. Without going into any more detail, the Baron was arrested and is now in a secure prison awaiting trial.

"Baron Gelding used this alias when mixing with the horse racing fraternity, but also went under the name of Baron de Buena in all his other criminal activities. He was the criminal mastermind of a large empire.

"I had a call from General Couture this morning to say the police have discovered his true identity."

"At this point an audible gasp came from Sir Martin, but I continued as though I hadn't heard it.

"This person is of great intelligence and gained a first class honours from Oxford and then went on to receive a doctorate in chemistry. He then relocated to Portugal where he started his criminal activities of drug smuggling, theft of racehorses, extortion and became massively wealthy. His name is Dr. Colin Nash, the elder brother of Sir Martin.

"It was Dr. Colin Nash who exerted intolerable pressure on Lord Percy by his blackmail demands that he should receive the whole of the proceeds of eighteen of Lord Percy's paintings of the Pyrenees every year. As the value of the paintings increased year by year, this helped Dr. Colin enormously by giving him much greater financial power to expand his criminal dealings.

"It was Dr. Colin who collected the two paintings, where the proceeds were hidden, from Sir Percy when he visited the orphanage at Lourdes and not a local dignitary as stated by Carolee. I'm convinced that Sir Martin was totally unaware of these blackmail demands and in no way would he have agreed to them.

"Carolee was aware from an early age who her father was and also her uncle and the reason she was living in an orphanage at Lourdes. It was only when she gained her mobility that her psychopathic mind really began to work and she joined her uncle in his enterprise.

"It was Carolee who thought up the plan for Sir Martin to woo Lady Helen so as to enable him to get employment at Peregrino Auction Services.

"Carolee was planning to fake paintings of some of the Old Masters and she realized that if he was an employee and a recognized art expert, no one would then query their authenticity if they were entered for auction by her father.

"Sir Colin gave Carolee the responsibility at Campan for the illegal production and sale of heroin to New York. Sir Martin, I am sure, had no wish to be connected with any of Carolee's planned illegal activities. I'm satisfied that Sir Martin had become completely bewitched by his daughter as though she had cast a magic spell over him to obey her every command."

"A fabricated story without proof, James, and I could sue you for slander," said Sir Martin.

"To continue, Carolee soon became a pathological liar. Sir Martin was also an excellent actor having once been President of the Oxford University Amateur Dramatic Society. It was easy for him to get the trust of Lady Helen in such a way. Similarly, it was easy for Carolee to put on a show of affection with words, being a born liar."

"The proof, James," repeated Sir Martin.

"It was only a few days ago, when I was analyzing in detail everything that had come to light during our investigation, that everything fell into place in my mind.

"Before our visit to Chantilly, I visited the home of Carolee's boyfriend, who became one of her victims. In the dining area, was an eighteenth century secretary writing desk. It was in perfect condition apart from some scratches down one side.

"On our return, I suddenly realized the possible importance of this. I'd seen an identical writing desk while at Cambridge with scratches in exactly the same place. These scratches were made by a person accessing the desk's secret drawer. I then went back to Dax's house to see if anything had been concealed.

"It was as I expected. Carolee was now a psychopathic serial killer. In the drawer, was a list of her killings to date and her future intended targets. There was also a memento from each of her victims."

"What did she take from Percy?" asked Lady Helen.

"It was a tie with the family crest. I'm sorry Lady Helen."

"Who else was on her list to kill?" asked Priscilla.

"Martin was to be her next victim, then Lady Helen, and then you," I said.

"In the secret drawer was also a notepad detailing all she'd done since she'd regained her mobility."

"What made her kill, James?" asked Lady Helen.

"Before we left for London, I asked General Couture to obtain her medical records from the local doctor in Lourdes. From an early age, the doctor had diagnosed her as a psychopath.

"This didn't worry him greatly as he was of the opinion that Carolee was being well looked after both by the orphanage and by her family. Little did the doctor know what was going on.

"He'd seen in Carolee a trait of manipulating others, her indifference towards responsibility, her impaired empathy, her inability to show remorse, her antisocial behaviour and the ease with which she lied.

"If brought up in a happy, caring family home, psychopaths usually lead a normal, fulfilling life. Violence rarely raises its head.

"There are no excuses for her actions as psychopaths are fully aware of what they're doing They have no value for human life and feel indifferent towards their victims."

""If only Percy had brought her home, everything might have been different. We would have given her the same love and affection as we give Priscilla," said Lady Helen.

"If so, Lady Helen, I'm sure you would have had another very highly acclaimed artist in the family.

"After arriving back in London I spent time obtaining further proof of what I'd learned.

"My first port of call was at the Mayfair Memorial Hospital where the matron, who was present at the births of Priscilla and Carolee, confirmed to me, as I've already told you, that Carolee had been born one day before Priscilla. She'd overheard what Sir Martin had said to Lord Percy about it being his responsibility to care for Carolee because of some financial dealings between their fathers. Martin insisted that the child should be brought up at an orphanage in Lourdes.

"Fortunately, the matron, Miss Nightingale, was travelling to see her sister in Paris the following day and promised Lord Percy that she'd be personally responsible for Carolee's journey to Lourdes and she would ensure that she'd be well taken care of.

"I then visited the registrars where indeed there was a birth registered in the names of Sir Martin Nash and Miss Cheetah one day before the birth of Priscilla. I had to obtain a court order to gain access to the name of the father as anonymity had been requested."

"So there's no doubt about my parentage?" asked Priscilla.

"None at all, my dear," I replied. "I then went to the law courts for confirmation of the court case between Lord Harry and Sir Martin's father which I have copies of."

"I hold my hands up, James, as you're correct in everything you've said," said Bigsby.

"That's our case concluded. Carolee was the murderer but she'd been deserted without family, without friends, confined in a wheelchair and with no one to turn to for the love and affection she must have craved so much. The despair and hopelessness she must have felt with only her painting for respite. It's no wonder her psychopathy turned into an evil desire to kill."

"Oh! If only parents would appreciate the wonderful gift of real family life and the blessing of having children," Bigsby said.

"Martin, you blackmailed Percy and betrayed the trust and affection I gave you," said Lady Helen. "You put intense pressure on my beloved first husband, yet through all the anguish he must have felt, he always made sure our life as a family was a very happy one. Lord Bigsby is correct in what he says. Family life is the bedrock of society.

"You were partly responsible for Percy's death by abandoning Carolee at birth. If you will please, collect your belongings, and then leave immediately afterwards, as I can no longer accept you as my husband.

"I believed you loved and cared for both myself and Priscilla in the same way that we both held great affection for you. I pray that you'll get your life back together again and, if so, I'll have a word with the Peregrino Auction Services to see if they will employ you in a less responsible position. It will be up to you then to prove your honesty and integrity in order to gain a more senior post.

"I'm sure without Carolee and your brother to tempt you into illegalities, you'll eventually be very successful as you certainly have supreme knowledge of the art world," said Lady Helen in a hushed voice.

Without a word, Sir Martin went upstairs to collect his possessions and an hour later, we heard the front door close.

EPILOGUE.

Everyone was silent for a long while until I spoke.

"I feel so sorry for everyone. As people say, 'If Only' but it seems especially applicable to the series of events we've now unraveled. After a period of reflection, we'll all have to get on with our lives. Tomorrow lunchtime, Lord Bigsby has arranged a special meal at The Club. I've invited a very pleasant young man who loves the countryside and the wildlife as an escort for Priscilla."

Priscilla blushed bright red, but I assured her that she would enjoy his company as both Lord Bigsby and I thought very highly of him.

"If you don't mind, I think Priscilla will feel freer to converse with the young gentleman if I'm not present so I'll make arrangements to go and see my solicitor while you're away. You both certainly deserve a special lunch and so does Priscilla and, what is more, I'll be settling the account for the meal," said Lady Helen.

"Thank you for your kindness, Lady Helen. I hope the meeting with your solicitor goes well. Lord Percy and Sir Clive had become very close friends. I hope you don't mind me asking if there's any way that it would be possible for Sir Clive to be able to breed horses again at Campan if the estate passes back into your hands, which I'm sure it will? I plead with you to allow him.

"When we saw him in prison, he was utterly broken. Without horses and animals and someone to turn to, he's not, psychologically, able to function. I can assure you, he's a very upright and honest man who wouldn't betray the trust of anyone. Jacques and Pierre, the previous farm managers, had a great respect for Lord Percy and they were in their element working with the animals and are also utterly trustworthy and conscientious."

"Don't worry, James, as I respect your advice."

"Well," Bigsby said, "we'll come for you at midday tomorrow, Priscilla, and we're looking forward to our meal immensely."

We arrived at The Club the following day for our lunch with Priscilla accompanying us. Neric was already waiting for us outside and greeted us all warmly. Priscilla was a little shy and nervous to begin with, but Neric soon had her at ease with his talk about the Pyrenees and the wildlife of the area. Before long, they looked as though they were old friends!

The meal was excellent as usual and enjoyed by all. Before we left, Neric made a date to meet up with Priscilla again. Bigsby and I remained at The Club for a while afterwards to properly celebrate our success and wonder what our next assignment would be. The following day, we heard that Clive had been released from prison and been allowed to return to his home. We were very happy for him.

A week later, Lady Helen came to The Club to pay for the cost of the expenses of the investigation and to thank us for leaving no stone unturned. She also gave us a little extra to buy a present for our wives.

After she'd left, Bigsby uttered in a grumbling voice, "My wife wants a new dining table and eight chairs from those exclusive cabinet makers in Park Lane. I suppose I have no excuse now after the gift we've received from Lady Helen for our investigations. Surely it would be much better spent on a few cases of wine from Chamour!"

"Well, My Lord, women are like fine wine. They get more expensive with age. Ha!"

We were eventually informed by General Couture that Dr. Colin Nash had been found guilty of four murders and had been sentenced to life imprisonment in a top security jail. He'd also been found guilty of drug smuggling, theft, fraud and blackmail. The four murders were the result of an unsuccessful revenge attack by a rival crime gang which Dr. Colin had been attempting to blackmail.

Marcos and Carlos informed the police of where Dr. Colin had buried the bodies at his Belgian stables. Marcos and Carlos had been employed by Dr. Colin for one year against their will as they were regarded as the best trainers in Europe. It was a tremendous relief for them to be free from his grasp and to know their twelve month nightmare was over. They even asked General Couture to inform us that they'd made a special visit to Cognac to buy a bottle of spiritus delikatesowy as a memento!

As soon as Clive heard about this, he invited both Carlos and Marcos to work with him at Campan.

Twelve months later, a letter arrived at The Club, addressed to myself and Bigsby, from Toulouse. What a lovely surprise we had to receive—an invitation, along with our wives, to the wedding of Priscilla and Neric. We were delighted for them. At the bottom of the letter was a note for Bigsby telling him that all the wine supplied at the wedding would be entirely from the vineyards of Chamour and free of charge!

There was a further letter from Lady Helen relating to us their news of the past year. She'd sold her house in London to live on the Campan Estate where she said she was enjoying life so much. She had contacted Sir Clive to start again the horse breeding side of the Estate and, needless to say, he was euphoric.

With Sir Clive's enthusiasm, Lady Helen soon became engrossed with horses and a platonic friendship had formed between them. They could often be seen on their horses riding in the countryside. Jacques and Pierre were back working on the farm and were very grateful to have been asked to work there again.

We were most delighted with the forthcoming wedding of Neric and Priscilla. With their joint love of the countryside, their friendship had quickly blossomed. Neric had left the employ of his father to take up the management of Chamour with the help of Priscilla. Both the properties that Lord Percy had bought in the Pyrenees were now lived in by the family. As we both had said, 'If Only'.

THE END

ABOUT THE AUTHOR

 David Wilson lives with his wife, Tess, and collie-dog, Millie, in a small village in Wester-Ross on the north-west coast of Scotland. They are surrounded by beautiful scenery. Deer and rabbits roam in the garden.

Wilson's interests are photography, landscape painting, fishing the hill lochs and walking in the countryside with his wife and dog.

Lately, with his wife, he had a small craft business. Also they operated a Bed and Breakfast establishment where they met guests of various nationalities.

He is now concentrating more on writing which he finds very enlightening. He also enjoys researching where he's able to increase his knowledge.

Made in the USA
Monee, IL
08 February 2020